You're Grounded for LIFE!

And 49 Other Crazy Things Parents Say

Joey O'Connor

Fleming H. Revell
A Division of Baker Book House Co
Grand Rapids, Michigan 49516

© 1995 by Joey O'Connor

Published by Fleming H. Revell
a division of Baker Book House Company
P.O. Box 6287, Grand Rapids, MI 49516-6287

Fifth printing, April 1997

Printed in the United States of America

Library of Congress Cataloging-in-Publication Data

O'Connor, Joey, 1964– .
    You're grounded for life! and 49 other crazy things parents say / Joey
O'Connor.
        p. cm.
    ISBN 0-8007-5549-9
    1. Parent and child–Religious aspects–Juvenile literature. 2. Child
rearing–Religious aspects–Juvenile literature. [1. Parent and child. 2.
Conduct of life. 3. Christian life.] I. Title.
HQ772.5.O25 1995
248.8'3–dc20   94-31929

Unless otherwise marked, Scripture quotations are from the HOLY BIBLE,
NEW INTERNATIONAL VERSION®. NIV ®. Copyright © 1973, 1978, 1984
by International Bible Society. Used by permission of Zondervan Publishing
House. All rights reserved.

For current information about all releases from Baker Book House, visit our web site:
http://www.bakerbooks.com

This book is dedicated to the O'Connor Family

Many Irish blessings to Dad, Mom, Colleen, Buddy, Rose, Kaki, Tata, and Newly for so many wonderful memories growing up.

I promise not to start any more fights, ditch my Dish Night by spending an hour in the bathroom, throw up after eating too many donuts at YMCA Indian Guides, scheme up new pranks (fingers crossed) or . . . light any fires.

Special thanks to Jodi Ferro and Carmen Fusco for their help in brainstorming all the crazy things that parents say!

Contents

Foreword   9

1. Look Both Ways! *Caution*   11
2. What Part of No Didn't You Understand?
   Accepting the Negative   15
3. Don't Make Me Stop This Car! *Fighting*   20
4. You Don't Really Mean That! *The Tongue*   24
5. Because I Said So! *Listening to Your Parents*   28
6. This Hurts Me More than It Hurts You!
   Punishment   31
7. I Don't Like Your Attitude! *Attitudes*   34
8. Clean Your Room. . . . It Looks Like a Pigsty. . . . Were You
   Born in a Barn? *Faithfulness*   38
9. You're Grounded for Life! *Restriction*   41
10. Someday, When You're Older, You'll Understand!
    Understanding   44
11. It's Not That I Don't Trust YOU–I Don't Trust OTHERS!
    Trust   47
12. You're Not Going Anywhere Until Your Room Is Clean!
    Choices   51
13. Will There Be Any Chaperones at the Party? *Partying*   55
14. One Day You'll Come Home and I Won't Be Here!
    Frustration   59
15. That Phone Is Going to Have to Be Surgically Removed from
    Your Ear! *Priorities*   62
16. If You Don't Shape Up, I'll Send You to Military School!
    Warnings   66
17. I Don't Like Your Choice of Friends! *Friendship*   69
18. Don't Do "IT!" *Premarital Sex*   74
19. Don't Take the Car–You'll Kill Yourself! *Safe Living*   77
20. As Long As You're Living under This Roof, You'll Do As I
    Say! *Family Rules*   81
21. Call If You're Going to Be Late! *Communication*   84
22. You'd Better Watch the Tone of Your Voice, Young Lady!
    Disrespect   87

8

23. Do That One More Time and Your Name Is Mud!
    Pushing the Limit   91
24. You'll Be Sorry! *Regret*   95
25. Stop Your Crying or I'll Really Give You Something to Cry
    About! *Complaining*   98
26. Just Wait Until You're a Parent Someday! *Parenting*   101
27. You'll Do It in My Time, Not Yours! *Honoring*   104
28. You Will Never Say That Word Again in this House! . . . Do
    You Understand Me? *Profanity*   107
29. Eat Your Dinner. . . . There Are Starving Kids in the World!
    Thankfulness   110
30. Do I Look Like I'm Made Out of Money? *Money*   113
31. I'll Be Right Back! *Patience*   118
32. If I've Told You Once, I've Told You a Thousand Times:
    You're NOT Going to the Rock Concert, AND THAT'S
    FINAL! *Accepting Defeat*   121
33. Turn Down That Music! *Rock Music*   125
34. What Do You Think I Am . . . Stupid? *Schemes*   129
35. Don't Tell Me–Ask Me! *Getting Permission*   133
36. Leave Your Little Brother Alone . . . He's Smaller than You!
    Example   136
37. When I Was a Kid, I Used to Walk Ten Miles to School . . .
    Exaggerations   140
38. Over My Dead Body! *Last Resorts*   143
39. Do You Have a Hearing Problem? *Listening to God*   148
40. I Know You Can Do Better than That! *Excellence*   151
41. I Know How You Feel. *Breaking Up*   155
42. We'll See. *Waiting*   159
43. Just Wait 'Til Your Father Gets Home! *Fear*   162
44. Would You Jump off a Bridge If Everyone Else Was Doing It?
    Peer Pressure   166
45. Don't Forget to Brush Your Teeth and Floss. *Discipline*   170
46. I Know You'll Make the Right Decision. *Confidence*   174
47. I'm Praying for You. *Prayer*   177
48. God Bless You. *Blessing*   181
49. I Believe in You. *Affirmation*   185
50. I Love You. *Love*   189

Foreword

I think Joey must have been looking in on my house when I was a teenager, or maybe he's right, most every kid in the world hears those same phrases.

I tried the line about walking twenty miles uphill (both ways) to school and back but my kids didn't buy it. Sometimes they don't even believe me when I say "This hurts me much more than it hurts you." My daughter Christy once said, after I used that line on her as my dad had on me, "That's the silliest statement I've ever heard come out of your mouth." I think she was mostly right.

On a more serious note, my mom died three months ago and the words in this book have really touched me. Some of the typical teenage hassles I had with her don't seem to matter now. I'm more aware than ever that God and family last. Can I be honest? I've forgotten most of my friends in junior high and high school except for my best friends and I don't see them anymore. However, whether we like it or not, our family stays with us, always.

You are making a smart decision to read and experience this book. It contains eternal truths that will affect your life for the positive, forever. I don't think you can read *You're Grounded for Life!: And 49 Other Crazy Things Parents Say* without its having a positive effect on your life.

If you've never had the privilege of meeting Joey O'Connor, you are missing out on a real pleasure. As you read this book you'll see he's fun, creative, a little wild and crazy, and he really knows how to communicate. One of the highlights of my life is having Joey for a friend and colleague as we attempt to make the world a better place. I know he's making a difference, and as you read this book so will you. God bless you.

Jim Burns, President
National Institute of Youth Ministry

Look Both Ways!

THE SITUATION

"LAAADDDYYY! Are you crazy! Whattaya trying to do . . . kill your kid?"

My mom recoiled in fear at the booming voice of the traffic officer.

"Can't you see? That light was red! Red! Red! Red! It can't get any redder! If you wouldda kept going in that crosswalk, you and your kid'd be dead by now!"

I was just a little kid, maybe four or five years old. My mom and I were late meeting my dad in downtown Los Angeles. We had taken a bus downtown in rush hour traffic and now, as we hurried to cross the street, my mom stepped off the curb pulling me in tow. *VVRROOOMMM!* A big truck barreled by and narrowly missed mashing us like an opossum roadkill on the side of the road. Across the street, a traffic officer blew his lungs out on his whistle, halting traffic. He marched over to my mom. Mom knew she was in trouble.

Dressed in a blue uniform with a shiny LAPD badge, the traffic officer with reflective, silver sunglasses proceeded to verbally rip my mom to shreds as I cowered and hid behind her legs.

"I should arrest you for child-endangerment! What kind of mother are you? Do you think I'm going to let people get killed on my shift? Everyone else stopped at the crosswalk. You got some kind of passport I don't know about? What makes you so important? Whattsamatter . . . you got some kind of death wish?"

My mom stood in front of the officer speechless. Embarrassed. With mouths gaping wide, bystanders watched in awe as the officer finished his forty lashes. Blowing his silver whistle again, the officer held up his white-gloved hand and stormed back across the street. Finally, the crosswalk sign turned green. Taking a deep breath, my mom looked down at me and nervously smiled, "Don't forget . . . look both ways."

THE SCRIPTURE

Above all else, guard your heart,
    for it is the wellspring of life.
Put away perversity from your mouth;
    keep corrupt talk far from your lips.
Let your eyes look straight ahead,
    fix your gaze directly before you.
Make level paths for your feet
    and take only ways that are firm.
Do not swerve to the right or the left;
    keep your foot from evil.
                    Proverbs 4:23–27

Look both ways. You've heard that saying ever since you were a little kid. Running out of the house with a red ball or bicycle, your mom and dad always warned you about the dangers of crossing the street. A little kid is no match for a two-ton hunk of high-speed steel. Looking both ways before you crossed the street not only kept you alive, but it also got you over to the park to play kickball with your friends.

You're not a little kid anymore. Nobody needs to tell you to look both ways before crossing the street. But now you face different dangers than you did as a kid. Dating. Friendships. Athletics. School. Drugs. Gangs. Future. Music. Movies. Parties. The list goes on and on. As a kid, you looked left and right before crossing the street. Now, as a teenager facing all sorts of difficult decisions, you need to look left, right, forward, backward, thirty degrees north, one hundred twenty-six degrees due east, up, down, over your shoulder, and under your feet. Being a kid was a whole lot easier than being a teenager.

Your parents want you to have a meaningful and satisfying life, and they resort to saying the same things over and over again so you don't forget the important lessons of life they're trying to teach you. Parents say the same crazy things again and again because, most of the time, they're looking both ways for you. Sure, not all parents are the greatest, but even if you have parents with big problems, at least you can learn from their mistakes.

Your mom and dad are trying to look both ways for you, and someone else is too. God is looking both ways for you. As crazy as it sounds, God sometimes uses your parents to teach you lessons he wants you to learn. *Sometimes God speaks through all those crazy things your parents say!*

God, as well as your parents, wants you to have a meaningful and satisfying life. He's provided a way for you to experience all the adventure that life has to offer through giving you the chance to know his Son, Jesus Christ. God has also provided you his Word as a road map for this life so you can know when and where to look both ways. The first thing you need to do is to guard your heart. That's why God says not to swerve to the left or to the right, but to look straight ahead.

14

Looking straight ahead will keep you on the exciting adventure God has prepared for you.

THE STRATEGY

Write down three to five of the craziest things your parents have ever said to you—the ones they say to you over and over again. After you have listed your crazy parent-sayings, write down what you think they're really trying to say. How does God use your parents to teach you things about this life? What lessons have you learned from your parents that might be the same lessons God wants you to learn?

Examples of crazy parent-sayings:

"Don't sit so close to the TV . . . you'll go blind!"
"How come you don't treat your friends like you treat your poor mother?"

2 | Accepting the Negative

What Part of No Didn't You Understand?

THE SITUATION

For many teenagers, *no* is an atrocious, revolting, over-used, uncreative, burnt-out word parents whip out like a Colt .45 six-shooter to gun down a nagging, persistent teenager like yourself. Yes. No. Yes. No. Back and forth. Forth and back. *No* never means yes and *yes* never means no. If you're like most teenagers, *no* is a word you hate. This stinking little *no* word sounds the same in Spanish. If you stick out your front lip and make it sound nasally, you can also say it in French—*non*. For teenagers across all fifty states in America, *no* means a lot of things. *No* means you can't go out on Friday night. *No* means you have to study instead of talk on the phone. *No* means you have to finish your peas before you leave the table (or brussels sprouts . . . Which is worse? I don't no. Know?). *No* is the lame word that means plea rejected, request denied, and permission refused. *No* means no and that's that.

Growing up, whenever I heard my mom or dad use that awful two-letter word, I shifted my tactics to diversionary warfare. If my dad told me I couldn't go out to play with my friends, I'd go ask my mom. If she said that wonderful, sweet-smelling word *yes,* then, like any other obedient child, I would do as she said. *I wouldn't want to disobey!* With seven offspring using the diversionary warfare tactic every 3.5 minutes, Mom and Dad caught on to that ploy quicker than an intercepted pass. If caught in the middle of inflicting diversionary warfare on my parents, my lightning-like escape route was a new round of tactics. While some of these worked, others backfired horribly. (Use at your own risk. I assume no responsibility for your mistakes!)

- I promise I'll finish my chores.
- How come I'm the only one who never gets to do anything?
- I always do everything you ask me to do.
- Don't you like me?
- I promise I'll never beat up all of my five sisters at once.
- I never do anything wrong and this is what I get in return?
- I'll run away.
- How would you like it if I always said no to you?
- I'll get off your back if you just say yes.
- I won't accept no for an answer.

THE SCRIPTURE

> As the heavens are higher than the earth,
> so are my ways higher than your ways
> and my thoughts than your thoughts.
> Isaiah 55:9

Why do moms and dads use the *no* word on you? As hard as it is to hear this awful word, learning to understand why parents say "N-O" can help you learn about life in all sorts of ways. Parents say no for many of the same reasons God says no. If you want to take the car on Saturday night but don't know about the incoming storm, as your dad does, do you think he'll give you the keys? If you had never seen a light socket before and wanted to stick scissors in one, do you think your parents would hand you the scissors? A major reason parents say no is to keep you from getting hurt. Making sure you are safe is a major lesson your parents studied long ago in Parenting 101. God wants you to live a long life, and he uses your parents to keep you safe. What's safe to you and what's safe to your parents is often a major point of disagreement, but let's just say your parents would prefer seeing you walk instead of pushing your wheelchair for the rest of their lives.

There are also a number of other good reasons parents say no instead of yes. *Reason #1: Life doesn't always say yes.* Young people who hear yes all the time and never hear no are rudely disappointed when they enter the real world. Parents who teach their children the meaning of the word *no* are actively preparing them for what reality will eventually teach them later. Teachers say no. College admission offices say no. Managers at work say no. No matter where you go in life, you'll quickly discover that *no* is a part of everyone's vocabulary. Parents hear the word all the time. Life doesn't always say yes. Remember that and you'll be able to accept the reality of no.

Reason #2: Learning to accept no builds character. "Delayed gratification" is a phrase psychologists use to explain what patience is. Translated into English, delayed gratification simply means to wait. When you delay your gratification, it means you get what you want later instead of now. Parents can't always fulfill your immediate requests. Learning to wait develops patience. Accepting the *no* word develops character. Understanding that you don't need everything the second you want it helps you grow up. Have you ever seen a three-year-old in a supermarket having a frenzied temper tantrum, kicking, screaming, biting, and clawing, all because his mother told him he couldn't have a candy bar? Delayed gratification isn't always a sweet and simple process. Learning to accept no for an answer teaches you that the world doesn't spin on your axis. Try explaining that to a three-year-old.

Reason #3: No *can protect you from the dangers of* yes. I had a friend in high school whose parents let him do anything he wanted. They lavished money, cars, and an assortment of other toys on him. *No* wasn't in their vocabulary. His first car accident in his BMW didn't send a warning signal to him or his parents. Since the car was totaled, they bought him another brand-new BMW. Not a bad prize for beating death. The only problem is that people don't have nine lives like cats do. My friend is now dead. He didn't even live to see the age of twenty. He lived on the dangerous side of yes because he never heard the caution side of no. Too much of yes, like anything, can be deadly.

Sometimes we can't understand why God says the things that he says, because he's too radical for us. After all, he is God. His thoughts are higher than our thoughts and his way of operating is different from ours. *No* is part of God's vocabulary—for his good, and for our good. God wants what is best for us. He doesn't want to see us hurt or humiliated by our bad decisions. God says no because he knows that the *yes* word isn't always the best thing for us.

THE STRATEGY

Take a few minutes to try to understand why your mom or dad tell you no. Before talking with them, spend a few minutes praying about how you can better understand your parents. Ask God to give you patience and the right words to say. Be prepared for answers you've heard before, but look for new ways to understand what they're saying and why. Without having any requests or favors in mind, ask them to discuss these questions with you:

1. What are the reasons why you might say no to one of my requests?
2. Are there things that I do that influence your decision to say no?
3. When you were a teenager, how did you respond when your parents said no to something you wanted to do?
4. Are there things I can do to get a yes answer instead of a no?

3 | Fighting

Don't Make Me Stop This Car!

THE SITUATION

Nine people. One red station wagon with fake wood on the sides. Two parents. Seven screaming, scratching, slapping, crying, fighting children. Driver's Ed doesn't have anything in the manual about trying to drive as a parent with seven hysterical kids in the car. This is a harsh lesson learned only in the fast lane of life. Attempting to both drive the car and scream into the rearview mirror was a difficult task for my folks. I don't know what the rearview mirrors are like in your family's car, but the rearview mirrors in the station wagon I grew up with had the strange capacity to make my parents look like demons. Anybody passing us on the freeway steered clear of the O'Connor station wagon. Why? A station wagon filled with kids fighting over broken crayons, scratched arms, pulled hair, and stolen dolls is the most dangerous car on the road. I can't understand how my parents can still live as normal human beings after spending years driving the seven of us all over town. If I had been my parents, I would have bought a moving van, thrown every one of us kids in the back, turned up the radio, and let the bumps, hills, and curves straighten us out.

When my sisters, brother, and I were driving our parents insane, the one line that applied to each sibling of the O'Connor Seven was a very clear, serious warning dealt by my dad: *"Don't make me stop this car!"* My dad, a very patient man, when pushed to his limit had the magical ability to make each of us believe we had the personal power to make him slam on the brakes. "Don't make me stop this car" was a last resort he generously offered before changing lanes and slowing down the station wagon. When the station wagon came to a complete stop at the curb, my dad would put the car in park and slowly turn his head to stare at seven very silent children. A stolen, broken crayon suddenly didn't seem so important anymore. "Here, you can have it back."

THE SCRIPTURE

If it is possible, as far as it depends on you, live at peace with everyone.

Romans 12:18

Making your parents stop the car is serious business. Whatever you do in life, *do not make your mom or dad stop the car.* I made my parents stop the car when I was a kid, and I'm amazed that I lived to tell about it. Winning a fight is not worth the price you will pay for pushing your parents to their breaking point. Neither God nor your parents want you to be a prizefighter.

Even so, God knows that you're going to get in arguments with the people in your family. That's why he said three very important things: (1) *If it is possible* ... You may live in a family where people like to fight. Some people would rather argue over a "borrowed" blouse that got stained than throw it in the washer to have it get unstained. Fights only cause headaches, hassles, and hurt feelings. Fights are what make

Mom and Dad pull the car to the side of the road. If it's possible to avoid getting in a fight, God says, "Avoid it."

(2) *As far as it depends on you . . .* When you're in a fight with your brother or sister, you have a choice to make: Break it up or keep swinging. My parents always said, "It takes two to make a fight." (And seven to create a brawl!) Stuff like holding back an unkind word, walking away, ignoring the terrible taunts of your older brother, and choosing to be a peacemaker instead of a troublemaker are a few ways to defuse a brewing battle. Most fights depend on your decision whether to wage war or not. God is depending on you to make the right choice.

(3) *Live at peace with everyone.* Everyone. That includes your parents. Your brother. Your sister. Your step-dad. Your step-mom. God has designed you to live at peace in his peace. Fighting is not in his game plan for your life. He wants you to be a peacemaker in your family. Choosing to live his way by refusing to be the next Muhammed Ali is the life Jesus wants you to live. Living at peace with everyone in your family doesn't mean you'll never have conflict or disagreements. Problems can have peaceful solutions. But if winning is everything to you, just wait until the station wagon comes to a complete stop.

THE STRATEGY

If you've blown it by fighting with your brother, sister, mom, or dad, the best and hardest thing to do is to say you're sorry. Take some time to read the following verses about forgiveness. Memorize Romans 12:18 in order to avoid future battles. Ask God for the strength to admit your faults to him and to the person that you hurt. Whether you started the fight or not, go to that person and ask for forgiveness. Go for a drive and spend some time screaming, "Don't make me stop this car! Don't make me stop this car!"

If we confess our sins, he is faithful and just and will forgive us our sins and purify us from all unrighteousness.

1 John 1:9

Therefore, if you are offering your gift at the altar and there remember that your brother has something against you, leave your gift there in front of the altar. First go and be reconciled to your brother; then come and offer your gift.

Matthew 5:23–24

For if you forgive men when they sin against you, your heavenly Father will also forgive you. But if you do not forgive men their sins, your Father will not forgive your sins.

Matthew 6:14–15

4 | The Tongue

You Don't Really Mean That!

THE SITUATION

A few years ago, my dad, my brother Neil, and I traveled through Europe for three weeks. On the train from Italy to Austria, three American females boarded our train and sat directly behind us: a grandma, mother, and daughter. The daughter, a fifteen-ish gem of a princess, the kind of girl you want to take on every family vacation, was not in a very good mood. She was upset, unhappy, troubled—out of control. The gentle, loving conversation among mother, daughter, and grandma went something like this:

"I hate you, Mother," cried the girl.

"Oh, you don't really mean that," countered grandma.

"Yes I do! I'm sick of this vacation! I want to go home!"

"Your attitude this whole trip has been awful," mother fired back.

My eyes met Neil's. Trying not to burst into laughter, we widened our eyes and gave each other a big, silent, *"Ooow!"*

Peeking over our chairs, we watched the American Gladiators wage World War III.

The girl wouldn't stop. "You've been mean to me this whole trip! I can't stand you!"

Grandma played referee. "Now don't say that, dear. You don't hate your mother . . . you really don't mean that!"

"Oh yes I do! You're the worst mother in the whole world! I hate you!" cried the girl, now in tears.

"And you're the most ungrateful teenager I've ever known," her mom spit back.

By this time, Neil and I were doubled over in our seats, laughing and making all sorts of horrendous faces. My dad wasn't laughing. Shooting out of his seat, he leaned over the back and said in a loud voice, "Would the three of you please be quiet? We don't want to listen to all of your squabbling!" Neil and I were now in tears, laughing hysterically, high-fiving each other, cheering, "Go, Dad!"

It wasn't over. Grandma continued, "Now apologize to your mother. You don't really mean those things you said."

"Oh yes I do and I'm not apologizing to her. She should apologize to me. And I don't care what that stupid man says!"

Neil and I howled like coyotes at the moon as the Wicked Witch of the West sputtered on. Did she really mean what she just said about that "stupid man?"

THE SCRIPTURE

> Reckless words pierce like a sword,
>   but the tongue of the wise brings healing.
>   Proverbs 12:18

When was the last time you were relentlessly reckless in saying something you didn't really mean? How many times have you lobbed an endless barrage of cluster bomb words, only to silently say to yourself after the damage was done, "Uh-oh. I wish I wouldn't have said that."

In fits of rage and frustration we have all said things we've come to regret. Reckless words do pierce like sharp, double-edged, serrated swords. Reckless words take dead aim and usually don't miss. Even though Neil and I laughed at the situation on the train (which did nothing to help anyone), God wasn't laughing, and neither was that grandma, mother, or daughter. Reckless words wound and destroy the people we love the most. And that's nothing to laugh about. I know . . . I've said a lot of things I didn't really mean.

Growing up with five sisters and one brother, I fired my mouth in all directions. Whether it was calling one of my sisters an ugly-no-good-dateless-foul-smelling-lower-life-form or taunting and teasing my little brother into a tantrum, my sharp words produced more holes than healing.

God's Word reminds us that we often don't mean what we say. But better yet, the Bible nudges, pushes, and helps us to say "I'm sorry" after we've stabbed with our tongue-shaped swords. After giving your mom or brother a verbal backhand to the heart, you can be wise with your tongue by following through with an apology and a renewed promise to watch what you say. Why? Because God's way is the wise way. God's way brings healing to hurting hearts.

Is it difficult to hold your tongue? You bet it is. Do you start every fight and disagreement in your family? I doubt it. You see, even when the fight isn't your fault, you still have the choice to control that wet, little muscle in your mouth that spits poison like a ticked off dilaphosaurus. God's wisdom can turn your tongue into a tool for his healing instead of a piercing sword for saying things you don't really mean.

THE STRATEGY

Saying things you don't really mean produces a lot of pain for you and the person you said them to. You can learn to tame your tongue by putting God's Word into practice. That's where James 3 comes in handy. Open your Bible and read

James 3:2–13. James tells us why it's so hard to tame the tongue and what the consequences can be for ignoring God's advice. As you read and study this Scripture, think about these questions that are designed to help you tame your tongue so you can be the person of wisdom and healing God has designed you to be.

1. How does James describe "a perfect person?"
2. What do bits on horses, rudders on ships, and small sparks have in common with our tongues?
3. What is the devastating impact of a raging fire? What are some similar results of how we use our tongues? Can you think of a recent example?
4. What do you think God thinks when we praise him and then say something mean to someone made in his image? How does God feel? How does that person feel?
5. Read verse 13. How can you be wise and understanding? Today, what are a few practical ways that you can use wise words instead of piercing words? Do you need to ask for someone's forgiveness for saying something hurtful?

Because I Said So!

THE SITUATION

You are probably one of the world's best philosophy students. Your insightful, inquisitive, highly interactive mind is always asking the basic philosophical question, "Why?" This simple, three-letter word drives your mom and dad bonkers.

"Why can't I go to Bob's house tomorrow?"

"Why am I the only one who never gets to do anything in this house?"

"Why do we always have to do things as a family?"

"Why is this stew cold?"

"Why can't I borrow the car Friday night?"

"Why do I have to wait for you to decide? Can't you just give me an answer now?"

"Why are you two so old-fashioned?"

"Why can't I wear this outfit? Everyone else dresses like this!"

"Why are you so paranoid about my going away for the weekend?"

"Why don't you ever hear my side of the story?"
"Why do you always tell me to stop asking you 'why?'"

Why? Why? Why? Some of these questions rank right up there with some of life's other most difficult questions, like "Why do minimarts that are open twenty-four hours a day and three hundred sixty-five days a year have locks on the doors?" and "Why do people collect hubcaps and Barbie dolls?"

Your intelligent mind is like a sharply honed, shimmering samurai sword, ready to engage your parents' meager attempts to defend their position. Like a diamond-bladed concrete cutter, you are prepared to slice through the soft slab of their feeble reasoning as if it were a bologna sandwich. Yet, your philosophical advances are cut short by four words parents pull out like silver bullets for a werewolf: *Because I said so.*

THE SCRIPTURE

Listen, my son, to your father's instruction
and do not forsake your mother's teaching.
Proverbs 1:8

Generally speaking, the *why* question is a good question, and *because I said so* is not a very good response. So WHY do parents say "Because I said so?" It's because parents are sick of the *why* question. *Because I said so* is the monotone, emotionless reaction to the endless barrage of *why* questions.

Your folks resort to *because I said so* when they feel as if you aren't listening to them. It's their way of saying, "I give up, but I won't give in." It's an easy way to terminate what they feel is a one-way conversation. Parents end conversations if they sense you're using the conversation to give a concussion rather than to have a discussion. Your parents may perceive your *whys* to be like the rapid-fire staccato of a semi-automatic machine gun. Your folks don't want to be shot down any more than you do.

Getting an intelligent response out of your parents and having an opportunity to explain your position can happen if you first listen to what they have to say. Listening to your parents shows respect for them and earns respect for you. You show your folks that you can handle situations in a mature way. Listening doesn't rule out conflict, but it does provide a bridge for two-way communication so the conflict can be resolved.

Our relationship with God is much the same. He wants to protect us because he loves us, so sometimes he says "Because I said so," because he knows we're not going to listen to him. If we'd first listen to what he has to say, then maybe we wouldn't need to ask, "Why?"

THE STRATEGY

You know your parents better than I do. What do you think are the roadblocks that get in the way of understanding them? Lack of listening to each other may be one of the roadblocks, but there could be others. List the topics that cause communication conflicts between you and your parents. Now write down what your parents most often say about these areas of your life. After doing this, write down what you think are the reasons for what they say. Then go talk to your mom or dad to see if you're on target with why they say what they say. Try to talk about things when there's no immediate problem. Listening to one another can pave the way for understanding one another in the future. For example, the areas my parents and I frequently argue about are dating, homework, and my friends:

Topic	What My Parents Say	Why?
Dating	"You can't date until you're sixteen."	They want to protect me.
Homework	"Do it before you go out tonight."	They want me to set priorities.
Friends	"Choose your friends wisely."	My cousin has awful friends.

6 Punishment

This Hurts Me More than It Hurts You!

THE SITUATION

Our parents didn't often have to resort to spanking us when we got into trouble. They were outnumbered: seven of us and two of them. There were plenty of times, however, when the O'Connor children, for any number of reasons, had to stand in the corner of the living room, face to the wall, sniveling and crying for being caught, sentenced, tried, and convicted. My parents used most of the usual child-rearing punishment techniques: going to bed without dinner; being grounded; extra chores; loss of allowance; no TV; sending us to our bedroom to think about what we just did. What were we supposed to do? Sit in bed and act like Winnie the Pooh? Think! Think! Think!

After separating two frenzied, hair-pulling, arm-swinging, hand-slapping, feet-kicking, nail-scratching, name-calling, threat-making, Tasmanian devil O'Connor kids fighting over who really won the last round of Candyland, our parents would always say the same familiar words as they dealt out punishment. You know what they are. I don't have to repeat them for you.

Now that I'm a writer, I have the privilege of sharing the worst case of parental punishment injustice ever. My appeals are still pending in the ancient halls of the U.S. Supreme Court. My oldest sister, Colleen, and I were the fighting equivalents of a cobra and a mongoose, a wolf and a snowshoe rabbit, a hawk and a fieldmouse. I was Godzilla and she was Tokyo. One morning before school, we got into a fight over something dumb (such as who had the worst morning breath). As we were screaming and slugging away at each other, my dad came in and broke it up. Tell me if you think this was a fair punishment: She had to miss one–(1), uno, I repeat, *one*–play practice; me?–I had my twelfth birthday party with all my buddies canceled! Is that cruel and unusual punishment or what?

THE SCRIPTURE

> But he was pierced for our transgressions,
>   he was crushed for our iniquities;
> the punishment that brought us peace was upon him,
>   and by his wounds we are healed.
> We all, like sheep, have gone astray,
>   each of us has turned to his own way;
> and the LORD has laid on him
>   the iniquity of us all.
>
> Isaiah 53:5–6

When you get grounded, your parents get grounded. When you get punished, your parents get punished too. Why is that? Because sin punishes everyone. Your parents did not raise you and your brothers and sisters to be kick boxers, heavyweight fighters, or WWF wrestlers. Nor did your parents ever want to be Tae Kwon Do referees, U.S. magistrate judges, public defenders, or prison wardens in their own home. When you fight, the whole family suffers.

Believe it or not, it's easier to receive a punishment than to give one. When you get grounded for slugging your sister in the arm, you're basically getting back what you dished out. But having to play prosecutor, judge, and jury in order to pass a fair sentence—that takes a lot more work, especially when you're sentencing someone you love. Punishing a teenager is not an easy thing to do.

God understands this punishment dilemma. He sees how each one of us has rebelled against him, yet because he loves us and wants to have an intimate relationship with us, he has chosen to place our punishment on his Son. Jesus Christ, God's only Son, was pierced for our sins and crushed for our rebellion against God. The punishment meant for us was given to him so that we could live. It is by the precious, sacrificial wounds of Jesus that we are healed. We were like a bunch of confused, lost, bleating sheep, but our heavenly Father punished his own Son instead of us. Punishment is always harder on the Father than it is on us.

THE STRATEGY

Take a few minutes to write a letter to God thanking him for not punishing you according to what your sins deserve. Thank him for Jesus, who loves you unconditionally and always welcomes you with his grace and forgiveness. Thank him for the Holy Spirit, who gives you the strength and will to follow Jesus every day. Ask God to give you the desire and strength to love him more than anything else. Read Isaiah 53:5–6 and think of all the ways God loved you enough to give you his Son so that you can know him personally.

7   *Attitudes*

I Don't Like Your Attitude!

THE SITUATION

Tomorrow is the anniversary of my best friend's death. Dana died after four years of a hard battle with cancer. So what does this have to do with attitudes, you ask? Read on.

In the short period of four years, my buddy Dana lost his father to a sudden death, lost the house he grew up in, saw all his possessions go up in smoke when an arsonist set fire to his garage, endured three major surgeries and numerous chemotherapy treatments, got ripped off in a health insurance scam, and had his Toyota 4 x 4 truck stolen—*twice!*

Facing tremendous financial, physical, and emotional strain, Dana never once cursed God or demonstrated a lousy attitude. As a friendly, always-smiling surfer, Dana inspired countless students in our high school ministry. His work as a paramedic focused on helping and serving others. On his days off, he'd pile students in his truck to take them surfing and boogie boarding. As most people who knew him would agree, Dana spent his life serving others instead of complaining about his circumstances. What a difference attitude makes!

Dana chose his attitude very carefully. If anyone had a reason to grumble and whine, it was Dana. Even though the rest of his life was in chaos and there was nothing he could do to control the cancer in his body, the one area in his life he could control was his attitude. By choosing how to think about and respond to his struggles, Dana was freed from being controlled by his circumstances. His attitude gave him more freedom than anyone I've ever known. Dana knew that attitude was everything.

THE SCRIPTURE

> You were taught, with regard to your former way of life, to put off your old self, which is being corrupted by its deceitful desires; to be made new in the attitude of your minds; and to put on the new self, created to be like God in true righteousness and holiness.
>
> Ephesians 4:22–24

There are all sorts of things that can contribute to having a bad attitude: You study really hard for a vocabulary test and end up with a C-; you play terribly at basketball practice; your boss at work yells at you for something someone else did; you find out your best friend was talking behind your back. And it really doesn't help much when your parents tell you how much they don't like your attitude! Circumstances like these can make you feel like a dark rain cloud is hanging over your head and the only one you can relate to is Winnie the Pooh's friend Eeyore: "Don't worry 'bout me, I'll be fine. No candles, no cake. Happy Birthday."

Even though your circumstances may stink, I believe each one of us has the choice whether or not to have rain clouds over us. If you have rain clouds over your head, it's because you have chosen them to be there. That doesn't mean you're an awful person; it just means that you choose what attitude you're going to live with. You also decide if you're going to inflict a bad attitude on others. You know how it goes: *If I'm going to be miserable, then I'm going to make everyone around me miserable!* You and I live or die by our attitudes. What kinds of attitudes do you choose to live by?

As followers of Jesus Christ, God calls us to put off our old self and our old way of thinking. He says to be made new in the attitude of our minds, to put on the new self which is created to be like God. When we choose to live with Christ-like attitudes, then people will see the righteousness and holiness of God in our lives. When that happens, we'll be able to radiate the powerful light of God's love instead of drip the drizzly rain of our little dark rain clouds.

THE STRATEGY

Take an Attitude Check

Here are some "attitude check" questions that will help you to better understand how to choose good attitudes instead of being controlled by your circumstances:

What attitudes do you have the most trouble with?
What attitudes do you show to the various people in your life, such as your parents, teachers, coaches, friends, and bosses?
How does this Scripture challenge you to make better choices with your attitudes?
Whom do you most admire for having a positive attitude?
Who is someone you know who lives with a bad attitude?
What is it like being around someone who always has a bad attitude?
In what ways are you responsible for your own attitudes?

When you feel a bad attitude coming on, what positive
   choices do you have?
How do your attitudes have a positive or negative effect
   on others?
How do you think God can help you with your attitude?
What is a practical way to apply Ephesians 4:22–24 to
   your life today?

Faithfulness

Clean Your Room. ...It Looks Like a Pigsty....Were You Born in a Barn?

THE SITUATION

No, I wasn't born in a barn, but I definitely grew up in an animal house. Cleanliness was not next to godliness in our house any more than Spic was next to Span. Trying to keep my room clean, let alone anyone attempting to keep the whole house clean, was similar to raking leaves in the wind. Did my room ever look dirty? Yes. Was there wet, sticky, smelly mud and food slop all over the floor? No. Besides, even if there had been mud all over the place, pigs are happy in pigsties.

The tactic my dad used to send the fear of clean through our bones was a simple announcement called "Room Inspection." At the dinner table, all my dad had to do was boldly proclaim that tonight was the night for Room Inspection, and a THX-Lucas-Sound blast would roar through the halls . . . *dunt-dunt-DAAAA!!!* The dinner table would quickly be deserted as my brother, sisters, and I dashed to clean our bedrooms.

Grabbing an authentic Knights of Columbus silver sword from its ornately designed sheath, my dad became the suburban equivalent to Captain Hook. Shining sword in hand, my dad passed from one room to the next, high-pitched screams rushing ahead of him: "He's coming . . . he's coming to your room next!" The crew would man their battle stations to show the captain their immaculately cleaned bunks.

Quarters were bounced on beds. The white glove tested for any speck of dust. Toys off the floor, matching shoes on shelves, desks straightened, and clothes put away were all essential elements of Room Inspection protocol. Anyone foolish enough to be caught stuffing junk under the bed had to walk the plank.

THE SCRIPTURE

His master replied, "Well done, good and faithful servant! You have been faithful with a few things; I will put you in charge of many things. Come and share your master's happiness!"
Matthew 25:21

I don't know what your room looks like, nor do I think you want to be lumped into the stereotypical, faceless group of adolescents whose rooms are somewhere in between a stinking dump and a nuclear test site. If, however, you are like some teenagers whose #1 priority is to not give in to threats of impending Room Inspections, then perhaps your parents have accused you of living in animal-like conditions.

Faithfulness is an important principle in the Bible, which asks a simple question: Can this person be counted on? In Matthew 25 Jesus tells the story about a few guys who were put in charge of their master's money. One guy was a loath-some sloth who did nothing, and the other two invested the money in order to make more dinero for the master. The master was counting on each one to be faithful, but in the end only two showed their faithfulness–through their actions. That's the type of character Jesus wants to develop in each one of his followers. Faithfulness includes a lot more than just cleaning your room. Faithfulness has to do with earning respect, developing trust, practicing integrity, and keeping your word.

American Express says, "Membership has its privileges." In God's kingdom, *faithfulness* has its privileges too. Being faithful in little things, like cleaning your room, earns your parents' trust to let you borrow the car or stay out later for special events; it helps them be a little more flexible, since they've come to know you as a dependable person. More importantly, faithfulness to God is what keeps your relationship with Jesus Christ alive and growing.

STRATEGY

Clean your room.

9 Restriction

You're Grounded for Life!

THE SITUATION

Restriction. *Been there.*

There are a lot of things in this life that get grounded. Electricians. Heavy machinery. Airplanes during blizzards. Washers and dryers. And teenagers.

When you get nailed for getting in too late or get caught cheating on a test, there are two types of sentences. The first is a simple grounding. When you're simply grounded, it means you've got either home or bedroom duty. If your room is loaded with TV, VCR, cable channel, satellite dish, CD stereo, telephone with call waiting, FAX machine, personal computer with 1200 baud modem, you basically still have contact with the outside world.

But if you get grounded for life, you might as well kiss goodbye any hope of celebrating your 50th wedding anniversary. Grounded for life means life in your bedroom with no possibility of parole except bathroom privileges. Then you know things are going to get worse before they get better. You're history, cheese steak, dog meat, a goner, an object of ridicule at school, dust, in deep yogurt, busted, convicted, an outcast, a menace to society, and a forgotten lost soul amongst the shipwreck of humanity. Grounded for life is as far as you can imagine into the future. It is eternity times a million.

Grounded for life is no simple threat. It is a reality enforced by parents who lock you up and throw away the key. Grounded for life is the grandisimo way parents say, "Adios . . . hasta la bye-bye."

THE SCRIPTURE

Our fathers disciplined us for a little while as they thought best; but God disciplines us for our good, that we may share in his holiness.

Hebrews 12:10

OK, so you agree that being grounded for life is not the way you want to spend your next sixty years. You still want to get your driver's license, go to your senior prom, play sports, graduate, find a career, get married, and have 3.8 kids someday. Not being grounded for life will enable you to see the sunshine, hang out with friends, and enjoy some simple pleasures in life, *like getting out of your bedroom.*

Why do some parents go to such extremes when you fail to dump the trash after being asked four times to take it out? Why do parents impose sentences with no regard for your constitutional rights? What kind of parent would impose such stiff penalties on their own offspring? Even the Bible says that our fathers disciplined us for "a little while," but not for life!

Believe it or not, your parents have not been to the Harvard Correctional School of Adolescent Discipline and Development. God's Word says that most parents discipline their sons and daughters as they think best, which accounts for a significant margin of error. In other words, your parents may not be pros in the area of discipline, grounding, restriction, and the revoking of privileges. Your parents are in the position of disciplining you as they think best. That's not always an easy or fun position to be in.

How is God different from your parents? God disciplines you so that you can share in something very special: his holiness. Discipline has a lot more to do with giving direction than giving punishment. God disciplines you for your own good, so that you learn to walk in his ways and always follow him. God wants you to share in his holiness because he wants you to be "whole" in him. Discipline is a process by which you get rid of the things that make holes, so you can take on the characteristics of God that will make you whole. When you're whole, you'll never be restricted. Wholeness in Christ means freedom. Freedom from sin. Freedom from guilt and regret.

THE STRATEGY

Ten Grounded-for-Life Ideas

1. Paint your bedroom with 10,281 coats of paint.
2. Breed a herd of hamsters so they can gnaw through your bedroom wall and provide an escape route.
3. Organize your monster truck card collection.
4. Call a realtor and arrange for your parents' home to be sold.
5. Use your mattress as a boogie board to safely jump out the window.
6. Peel off the drywall and create a neo-construction decorating theme.
7. Start a Bedroom Sale mail-order business.
8. Join Inmates Anonymous.
9. Hold your little sister as a hostage to negotiate your release.
10. Read these verses about God's holiness to learn how God wants to share his holiness with you: Hebrews 12:14, Romans 6:22, Romans 12:1, 1 Corinthians 1:30, 1 Peter 1:15.

10   Under-standing

Someday, When You're Older, You'll Understand!

THE SITUATION

To this very day, there are a lot of things I don't understand. My parents always told me that someday, when I was older, I would understand everything they already understood. I'm still waiting. For instance, I still don't understand why my older sisters got to stay up later watching TV than I did. I still don't understand why, after Daylight Savings Time, I had to go to bed while it was still light outside. I still don't understand why I had to do yard work and housework, but my sisters only had to do housework. I still don't understand why my lovable, black Labrador, Big Joe, who terrorized the neighborhood, had to be given away. And I still don't understand why my dad *still* wears plaid pants and striped shirts.

You face the same sort of mind-boggling situations. One week, your parents let you borrow the car. The next week, they say you can't borrow the car. Your older sister was allowed to date at a young age, but now, when you want to go on a date, your parents say you're not old enough. You do all your chores, work hard to get decent grades, try to keep a good attitude so you can go skiing for the weekend with friends, but what do your parents say? N-O.

"What is there to understand," you ask? Are your parents just trying to buy time? Are they throwing curve balls because you have a low batting average? Are your parents a team of mad scientists and you're the lab rat? Is your life an excruciating experiment? Is this a cruel hoax? Why can't anyone give me a simple answer? You want a simple answer? I know what your parents will say!

THE SCRIPTURE

Consider it pure joy, my brothers, whenever you face trials of many kinds, because you know that the testing of your faith develops perseverance. Perseverance must finish its work so that you may be mature and complete, not lacking anything.

James 1:2–4

Not getting answers to simple questions can be a real test, a test of your character, a test of your will, a test of your attitude—and a test of your faith. Hearing from your parents that, someday, you'll understand why they think the way they do is the equivalent to hearing that someday there will be a cure for the common cold or a landing on Pluto. *Someday* is no day. *Someday* tests your faith *today.*

I still don't know why everyone else on the block got an ATC motorcycle, but I didn't. That was a test. You may not know why your parents have recently got a divorce. That's a really hard test. When faced with situations you don't understand or circumstances that have no simple answers, God's Word says to consider it pure joy, because the problems and struggles you endure test your faith and produce perseverance.

Why does God want to develop perseverance in you? God's process of perseverance develops maturity so that you will be complete in every area of your life. Parents sometimes think that maturity is something you arrive at when you're older, something you get *someday;* but God is in the process of making you mature today. As your faith is tested and perseverance is developed, maturity becomes the finished product. According to James, testing plus perseverance equals maturity. That's a solid answer you don't need to be older to understand.

THE STRATEGY

How are you supposed to handle conflicts with your parents when you don't understand where your parents are coming from? Here are people you can talk with to get their advice about how they'd handle the situation you're in:

Friends: What do your friends do when they don't understand their parents? Look for positive ways they handle misunderstandings, then learn from them.

Youth pastor: Talk to your youth pastor and see how he or she would handle your problem. Your youth pastor can give you some good advice, I hope.

Teacher: Teachers deal with parents and students all the time. Ask one of the teachers you trust how you can best understand your folks.

God: Spend some time talking to God about what you don't understand about your folks. Ask him what he is trying to teach you during this test. Pray for his wisdom to know what to say to your parents.

11   *Trust*

It's Not That I Don't Trust YOU— I Don't Trust OTHERS!

THE SITUATION

Yeah, right. The problem with getting permission to go out for the evening is that there are so many people in this world that your parents don't trust. Even though your parents explicitly say that they trust you, they certainly can come up with a bunch of "good" reasons why you should stay home tonight. Wacko reasons like: You need to attend a cousin's pet's funeral tomorrow. It's Friday the 13th. It's sprinkling rain. Planetary alignment is off. It's a bad day on the stock market. A DC-10 jet airliner might fall out of the sky and land on your car. Now aren't those good reasons for you to stay home tonight and enjoy a fun-filled evening with your family? Why would you want to go spend the evening with your friends when you can stay home with your little brother? Remember . . . your parents trust you . . . they just don't trust others. *Others* means everyone. According to Socratic logic, that means your parents don't trust anyone. Is this a basic trust issue or what?

When submitting my passport to my dad to go out for the evening, I could always expect to hear this classic line as I explained my way through the same questions you face every time you want to go out with friends. After sitting at a small table in a windowless, cold room with a bright, glaring light in my face and getting grilled with The Big Five Ws (Who, What, When, Where, and Why?), I usually passed his Border Patrol interrogations. I wondered, "Gosh, if my parents really trust me, why are they plugging at me with all these questions?"

THE SCRIPTURE

> Now it is required that those who have been given a trust must prove faithful.
>
> 1 Corinthians 4:2

If you get grilled every time you want to spend the evening at your friend's house, and you feel like your parents don't trust you or others, the real issue is just what you think it is: *trust*. Trust is the most important part of your relationship with your parents. Trust is the glue, cement, and industrial strength bondo that seals relationships. Can your parents trust you?

You are one of your parents' most important concerns. The invisible "others" your parents don't know are not. There are plenty of parents who have lost their children to other people. I know it sounds extreme, but your parents may have a healthy fear of the other people who are drunk drivers, gang members, rapists, lousy drivers, or otherwise dangerous. I'll say it again: You are one of your parents' most important concerns. Most parents don't trust the "others" they don't know. Would you?

If you wonder whether or not your parents trust you, ask yourself the simple question, What do I do to show that I'm worth trusting? "Now wait a minute," you may say. "If my parents really loved me, then they'd trust me no matter what." Not necessarily. Trust makes relationships work, but unlike God's unconditional love (which is free), trust is something you earn. You pay for trust by proving yourself faithful. If you want to earn your parents' trust, the Bible says to give some evidence that shows you are a faithful person. A simple definition of a faithful person is *someone who follows through.* Do you follow through on what you say you're going to do? Have you, in any way, shown your folks that they can't trust you? Having a good relationship with your folks is all about trust. Trust depends on you, not on "others."

THE STRATEGY

Remember when you were a little kid and your mom used to jot down all sorts of info for the babysitter? Well, to help build trust between you and your folks, so you can show them what an organized, efficient, thoroughly responsible teenager you are, see on the next page the new and improved teenage version of that info pad the babysitter never read in the first place. Before requesting permission to leave home for the evening, do your homework first by preparing all the information you know your dad's going to ask you anyway. Prove yourself to be trustworthy.

Permission to Leave Home Request Pad

Date: *February 19, 1995*

Time: *4:35 P.M.*

# of people I'm going with: ① 2 4 8 10 458 _____

Where we're going: Movies Mars Paris *Tom's House*

Phone #: *555-3478*

Who's going: Aerosmith/Wayne & Garth/ *Tom & I*

Who's driving: Elvis Presley/Mario Andretti/ *I am*

Model car/year:
- 1972 Late model Impala, two-door sedan, rust-colored
- Dad's 1957 vintage Rolls-Royce . . . **NOT!**
  Dad's green "bomb"

Driving record/DMV background check:

A-OK ✗ Fair__ Revoked__ Who Needs a License?__

E.T.A. at home: 10 P.M. 11 P.M. Midnight 2:46 A.M.

Sunup *tomorrow by noon*

Parents home? Yes ✗ No___

(If 'No' is checked, reason why?) *aliens got 'em!*

Alternate locations we'll be at: *mall, Eric's house*

CPR certification #, FAX #, School I.D. #, Car phone #,
Passport #, VISA/Mastercard/Discover #, Social
Security # ALL ON FILE!

Bob

12 Choices

You're Not Going Anywhere Until Your Room Is Clean!

THE SITUATION

Growing up, I was into dolls—manly dolls. Saturday morning would come around and I'd be sitting in front of the TV, legs crossed, major bedhead hairdo, chowing down on Peanut Butter Captain Crunch cereal. Even though I'd watch all my favorite Saturday morning cartoons like *Scooby Doo, The Jetsons, The Flintstones,* and *Sigmund the Sea Monster,* my favorite Saturday morning hero wasn't a cartoon character but a TV commercial figurine—a real Man-Doll, who was designed to shape the future masculinity of all six-year-old boys. . . . He was the man of all men, the hero of all heroes, the one who put all wannabe Chuck Norrises, Steven Segals, Rambos and Rambies to shame. . . . He has outlived He-man and Skeletor, Transformers, and Stretch Armstrongs. . . . He is the legendary American hero. . . . A stalwart man of bullet-proof character who has deflected more advances from that spoiled, Corvette-driving Barbie. . . . He is none other than GI Joe!

Nowadays, the GI Joes sold in stores are wimpy-size sissy dolls, but when I was a boy, GI Joe was man-size. I, GI Joey, had every GI Joe set imaginable: The Jungle Set complete with snakebite kit; The Egyptian Desert Explorer Set complete with yellow, six-wheel desert vehicle with winch on back to pick up mummy coffin; The Arctic Ski Patrol Set complete with a white powder suit, Rossignal skis, and Rayban sunglasses; The Navy Frogman Scuba Set complete with dive gear, ammobelts, and razor-sharp plastic knife.

After spending hours infiltrating enemy territories, blowing up clandestine airstrips, discovering mummified bodies, and skiing through subzero temperatures, I was ready to leave the chaotic mess in my bedroom and sneak outside to ride my bicycle. It didn't take long to be told that GI Joe was never allowed to go anywhere until his barracks were clean. GI Joe had a drill sergeant. My drill sergeant was my mom.

THE SCRIPTURE

And Jesus grew in wisdom and stature, and in favor with God and men.

Luke 2:52

Barring your exit from the house because of a messy room is just one tactic parents will use to help you understand how your freedom is related to your choices. A messy room is like a tracer bullet that follows you around until it hits its target: you! I know it's a hassle picking up smelly socks, half-eaten slices of pizza on greasy paper plates, piles of crumpled clothing, books, magazines, tennis shoes, and wadded paper balls from your Shakespeare essay revisions, but most moms refuse to be maids.

Did Jesus ever have a messy room? Did he ever have to make his bed, pick up his sandals, and hang up his tunic in his closet? No one really knows the answers to such intriguing questions, but the one thing the Bible tells us for certain is that Jesus had choices to make. And Jesus always made good choices.

You may be thinking, *Duh, of course Jesus made good choices. How hard is it to make good choices when you're perfect? Being God does have its advantages.* But what does the Scripture say? *Jesus grew in wisdom and stature.* Growing in wisdom is a process. Growing in stature not only involves physical growth, but more importantly, character growth. One of the results of growing in wisdom and stature is finding favor with God and other people, which includes your parents. Your growth is directly related to your choices.

When Jesus walked on this earth, even though his nature as God was perfect, Jesus was still a full-blown teenager for a time. He still went through the difficult process of growing up. Jesus had to make choices just like you do. That's why he understands when you struggle to make good choices, even simple ones like cleaning your room without your mom having to remind you. Good choices will take you somewhere, and bad choices will take you nowhere.

THE STRATEGY

If you want to find out the condition of the average teenager's bedroom, pick out a couple friends whose rooms you want to secretly videotape, then call their folks and tell them you want to come over to see how clean your friend keeps his or her room. If your friends are slobs, believe me, their parents will have no problem with your providing documented evidence. Select one person to be the reporter on location. Video the reporter leading you through the front door, into the house, and finally into your friend's room. Proceed to create a funny commentary on the condition of your friend's bedroom. Film the floor, bed, drawers, desk, closet, bathroom, and dresser. Be sure to get personal statements and interviews from parents and siblings. Show the video that week at your youth group meeting, at school, or at a party. You may even want to tape eight to ten bedrooms and host your own "Messy Bedroom Video" premiere. Have a blast, and don't forget to clean your room!

Will There Be Any Chaperones at the Party?

THE SITUATION

A few months ago I received a letter from Trevor, one of my former high school students, who is at college in San Diego. In the letter he wrote:

I'm meeting a lot of people who are not Christians, and somehow we always figure out where each other stands. It's exciting to put all my Christian beliefs to the test: things like patience, understanding, sharing my faith in God and trying not to be ashamed or hide what I value, i.e. Bible study, not partying, not swearing. One of my neighbors told me to go smoke a joint instead of going to Bible study last Tuesday. So standing firm and getting challenged are new and common things for me.

If you're a Christian facing difficult questions about what to do with the party scene in your town or on campus, here are a few facts to consider:

1. Drugs and alcohol will always be available.
2. You'll always find people to party with.
3. If you choose to use drugs, your relationship with God will suffer.
4. If you choose not to use drugs, your friendships may suffer.
5. If you go to parties and don't use drugs, you'll be challenged.
6. If you go to parties and use drugs, you won't be standing firm.
7. The decisions you make today will affect who you are tomorrow.

Just like Trevor said, getting challenged to party is a common thing for teenage Christians. But the real challenge is standing firm. When challenged, Trevor stood firm because he knew where he stood with God. Do you know where you stand?

THE SCRIPTURE

> Be self-controlled and alert. Your enemy the devil prowls around like a roaring lion looking for someone to devour. Resist him, standing firm in the faith, because you know that your brothers throughout the world are undergoing the same kind of sufferings.
>
> 1 Peter 5:8–9

It happens all the time. Friday, at school, a flyer is passed around letting everyone know of a kegger party with a live band this Saturday night. All your friends are talking about it, and even though you don't want to drink, you'd still like to have a fun time. Not admitting to your folks what you do know about the party, you waver back and forth in your mind how you're going to handle the inevitable question you know your mom is going to ask: "Will there be any chaperones at the party?"

Parents ask the chaperone question because they are more interested in your preservation than your popularity. Not only are your parents concerned about your well-being, but God is too. That's why he says to be self controlled and alert. Not only do drugs devour, but you also have an actual enemy who will try to devour you and your faith in Jesus Christ at any cost. Did you get that? *Satan will try to devour your faith at any cost.* Like a roaring lion, he is looking to make chopped liver out of your relationship with God.

Partying is just one of the tempting ways Satan will use to distract and devour you. Partying looks fun, attractive, mysterious, and alluring in a sneaky, rebellious type of way. Partying may look enticing, like a piece of poisoned bait, but afterward it leaves you feeling trapped and empty. If you want to stand firm in your faith, you need to stay alert to the traps Satan sets. At all costs, resist him and stand firm in Christ so you can experience all that God has for you. Partying will give you nothing and take everything. God will give you everything and take nothing. Stand firm!

THE STRATEGY

The best way to stand firm when you're facing the party challenge is to take a good, hard look at your friendships. *You will become like those you hang out with.* Here's a list of questions to help you evaluate your friendships in relation to partying:

Do your friends challenge you to party or challenge you to stand firm?

How do your friends react when you don't give in to their wishes?

What friends of yours drink and use drugs?

Where do you draw the line with your friends in regard to partying?

Do you know your friends' feelings about drugs and alcohol?

Would you still have your friends if you didn't party with them?

Are your friends out to change you for better or worse?

14 *Frustration*

One Day You'll Come Home and I Won't Be Here!

THE SITUATION

When was the last time you really frustrated your mom? Was it something you said, like complaining about her creative new French recipe, *eggplant extraordinaire?* Or did she get a sore throat from yelling at you, after telling you a hundred times, to do your own dishes? Maybe she waited in the parking lot at school for an hour because you forgot to call her and tell her you were getting a ride home from a friend? Perhaps she had a really lousy day cleaning the house, working a part-time job, and paying bills, and then you came home griping that there was nothing to eat in the fridge?

Frustrated with seven unappreciative and uncooperative kids, my mom would tell us, "I've just about had it. One day you'll come home and I won't be here. Some day I'm going to pack my suitcase and never come back." When my mom flipped her frustration switch, it wasn't a good idea to offer to help her pack. That's when Dad stepped in.

"All right, you kids. I want everyone in the living room in ten minutes for a Family Meeting." Family meetings meant trouble. Mom was about to lose it and we were about to get it. Colleen, Carolyn, Rosemary, Kathy, Joey, Loretta, and Neil were dust.

"OK, I want all of you to listen and listen very carefully. Your mother is not your maid. She is tired of all your complaining and bad attitudes. If you're going to be part of this family, then you're going to help out around here. And if you don't, then you're going to be in big trouble. There will be no allowances, after-school sports, play practices, or going over to your friends' houses. Do you understand me?" Pity the one who didn't understand.

THE SCRIPTURE

> Instead, whoever wants to become great among you must be your servant, and whoever wants to be first must be slave of all. For even the Son of Man did not come to be served, but to serve, and to give his life as a ransom for many.
>
> Mark 10:43–45

Being a mom is one of the most thankless jobs known to womankind. Not only did your mom go through labor pains for you, but she also endures the pains of grumpy moods and little to no appreciation for all her hard work. A mom's job description is endless: cook, cleaner, chauffeur, counselor, planner, shopper, organizer, coach, cheerleader, and candle-lighter for every birthday you have. Moms get burnt out just like you.

You can make a major difference in your mom's life by being a servant. In God's kingdom, being a servant is the most noble position you could ever aspire to. Being a servant is what Jesus calls you to be. Becoming a servant starts with simple ways of serving others. Instead of dropping your books and things on the kitchen counter when you walk in the door, put them in your room so your mom won't have to clear them off. Offer to do the dishes. Ask your mom if she needs help around the house. Pick her up from work so she doesn't have to wait for a ride home. Serving your mom will show her, by your actions, that you love and appreciate her.

Jesus said that he did not come to be served, but to serve. That's a great question to ask yourself: Are you here to be served or to serve? Serving is true greatness in the eyes of God. If you serve your mom around home, she'll never threaten to leave. She'll never want to leave.

THE STRATEGY

Mother's Day comes only once a year. Your mom needs more than one Mother's Day. Here are some ways you can surprise her any day of the year. Anything you do, whether simple or big, will be much better than doing nothing at all.

Make a "Happy Mother's Day" poster to use every time you surprise your mom.
Bring her flowers.
Clean the house.
Call her and tell her that you love her.
Take her out for a special meal together.
Create a fun date for your mom and dad.
Ask her what special project she wants done around the house.
Buy her favorite perfume.
Get her a gift certificate for her favorite store.
Take her to a play or concert.
Give her a weekend away.
Make dinner.
Help her in the garden.
Throw her a surprise party.

15 Priorities

That Phone Is Going to Have to Be Surgically Removed from Your Ear!

THE SITUATION

Alexander Graham Bell would have been proud of today's American teenager. His invention, the telephone, has provided a network for more teenagers than any other modern invention. Thanks to good ol' Alex, the telephone has helped millions of teenagers figure out homework assignments, avoid embarrassing face-to-face breakups with boyfriends and girlfriends, make weekend plans, ask someone out for a date, spread the latest news about the new guy on campus, help cheer up a friend who's feeling down, and figure out what to wear to school tomorrow.

Not only would Alex be proud about how much the telephone has helped meet a teenager's most vital communication needs, he'd be amazed at the latest telephone technology available to teenagers: call rudeness, er, call waiting; call forwarding; calling cards; personal 800 numbers; party lines; portable phones; speaker phones; and answering machines that record background stereo music so loud that a teenager has to scream into the machine in order to make a message—*HI, THIS IS J-A-A-K-E! LEAVE YOUR NAME AND NUMBER AND I'LL CALL YOU BACK AFTER I TURN DOWN MY GUNS & ROSES CD!!!*

While you're at home, the telephone is your only means of staying in touch with the real world. Your telephone is as vital to your social status as your ears are to hearing. Without a phone, you are out of touch, disconnected, and your life is indefinitely put on hold. Call 911.

THE SCRIPTURE

> The sluggard craves and gets nothing,
> but the desires of the diligent are fully satisfied.
> Proverbs 13:4

If your parents were given the chance, they might want to lynch Alexander Graham Bell. For some weird reason, when teenagers talk on the phone, parents get stressed out. They scream embarrassing orders while you're on the phone, making it clear that they're uptight about something remotely related to your phone usage: "Tell him to call back after dinner!" "Tell her to call you on your own phone." "How many times have I told you that I don't want you on the phone after nine o'clock?" "I don't want you on that phone until all your homework is done."

Besides worrying about having to pay medical bills for your cauliflower ear and your earwax removal kits, your folks are wondering if chemistry, English reports, history, test preparation, and part-time jobs are getting done. Even though they know that there's nothing intrinsically wrong or harmful about talking on the phone (unless you trip and get strangled by the cord), your parents want to make sure it isn't your top priority.

A common theme found in Scripture that relates to phone usage is the difference between a lazy person and a diligent person. When it comes to speaking into a banana-shaped high-tech instrument for three hours, your parents may wonder if you're being resourceful with your time. You may need to ask yourself these questions: Are you lazy or are you diligent? Do you spend more time talking on the phone than you do completing your homework? Have you first cleaned the kitchen, like you promised your mom, or have you spent the past forty-eight minutes talking about the dance last Friday night? If you're taking care of what's important first, then your folks probably won't mind as much when you're on the phone. In fact, they may even take back that silly threat about surgical phone removal.

THE STRATEGY

How much time do you spend on the phone? If it's more than a couple hours a night, not only do you want to consider buying stock in AT&T or MCI, but you may also want to look at the other obligations in your life. Take a piece of paper and write down how much time you spend each night on the phone. Now list all the responsibilities you have each week, like cleaning the barn, homework, lacrosse practice, volunteering time at a soup kitchen, washing clothes, cleaning out the hamster cage, youth group meetings, time with friends, etc. Circle your priorities and rank them in order of importance. Where do those hours on the phone each night rank?

Ask yourself, do I accomplish my most important goals before talking on the phone? Ask God to help you stick to your priorities before sticking your ear to the phone. He is always listening, ready to take your call.

16 Warnings

If You Don't Shape Up, I'll Send You to Military School!

THE SITUATION

In junior high, my best friend, Randy, and I used to do all sorts of crazy things together, which of course my editor will not allow me to sanction–but which I can *tell* you about! There was the time we almost blew out every window on the whole street by lighting an M-200 (half stick of dynamite). Or the Halloween when we were rearranging pumpkin faces with a baseball bat and got chased down the street by a crazed doctor. (None of us got caught except Mark Vallis's sister.) Or the time we smattered tomatoes and eggs on the inside of a girl's house when she opened the door. Or the time we launched water balloons two hundred yards onto sunbathing tourists at the beach and got chased by five mad, muscular marines from Camp Pendleton. Or the many times we threw tennis balls at the rent-a-cop security patrol car in our neighborhood.

In our home, when we were acting up Mom would threaten to send my sisters to the Ramona Convent and my brother and me to military school. *Who in the world would send their kid to military school?* I always thought to myself. The only reason I figured military school could come in handy was for new tactics and battle strategies against my sisters. Military school was the place to send the next George Patton, Douglas MacArthur, or Norman Schwarzkopf. Getting my head shaved and walking in formation dressed in uniform was nothing I wanted to get drafted for.

I got the news in the middle of summer after graduating from eighth grade. Randy told me we wouldn't be going to the same high school together. His parents were sick and tired of telling him to shape up. Randy was being sent to military school!

THE SCRIPTURE

Better a poor but wise youth than an old but foolish king who no longer knows how to take warning.

Ecclesiastes 4:13

I'm sure Randy got a few military school warnings. I had my fair share, but since my dad was a navy man, he probably didn't want to send me the army or marine route, and fortunately, there weren't any naval military schools near where we lived.

Knowing when and how to take a warning is an essential growing-up survival skill. Parents dish out warnings to get our attention. The idea is that if you don't fall in line at home, you'll definitely learn how to fall in line at military school—your drill sergeant will make sure of that. Your parents did not enlist to be your personal drill sergeant. Even though you may consider your parents to be covert military personnel, they probably don't enjoy badgering you to shape up or ship out.

God's Word encourages you to know how to take a warning at an early age because by the time you're old, it may be too late. As a teenager, you will occasionally mess up. I did all the time! The most important thing is to know how to respect your parents' warnings. You have the opportunity to listen and learn how to take a warning now. Randy got sent to military school, and it didn't do much to shape him up.

THE STRATEGY

Warnings have specific meanings and purposes. You'd probably be a little miffed and possibly be very frightened if you were crossing train tracks, the warning sign wasn't working, and a train was coming. God gives you all sorts of stop signs, flashing red lights, and barriers to keep you from harming yourself. Here are some questions to help you get wise when it comes to warnings:

> What different types of warning signs do you see every day?
> What is the purpose of a warning sign?
> What are the consequences when people do not obey warning signs?
> What kinds of warnings do your parents usually give you?
> Why are your parents warning you about certain attitudes or behavior?
> What kinds of warnings do you think God gives you?
> Why is God warning you about specific areas of your life?
> How can God's warnings help you to become wise?
> What is a warning that can help you keep your relationship with God strong?

I Don't Like Your Choice of Friends!

THE SITUATION

Some friends are not made for each other. There are all types of friendships, but the type of friendship that you want to be sure to avoid is the dangerous friendship. Dangerous friendships are when one "friend" pulls another friend in the wrong direction. Dangerous friendships are like mixing matches and gasoline—one spark and everyone gets torched.

Show me who your friends are and I can tell you whether or not they're dangerous. Dangerous friends pressure you to drink when you promised yourself you wouldn't: "Come on! One beer ain't going to hurt you!" Dangerous friends look out for their own interests instead of yours: "Why don't you want to make love? I've got a condom!" Dangerous friends play with death: "Let's see if your car will hit 100!" Dangerous friends play games that no one wins.

Working with hundreds of students the past ten years, I've seen many friendships destroyed because of one or two students being a negative influence on their other friends. Dropping acid, taking the car without asking, stealing car stereos, shoplifting in malls, joining a gang, running away and convincing a friend to do the same—friends who do these things are dangerous. Sure, you may want to hang around someone you think is cool, but it doesn't take much to see that a dangerous friendship is not a friendship at all. Danger is synonymous with rattlesnakes, toxic waste, coffins, snappy poodles, the running of the bulls in Pamplona, skydiving without a parachute, corned beef hash, and banana peels. Danger is something you want to avoid.

THE SCRIPTURE

> He who walks with the wise grows wise,
> but a companion of fools suffers harm.
> Proverbs 13:20

When your mom or dad tells you that they don't like your friends, what are they really saying? Do they have any specific reasons for not liking your friends?

Even though it may seem as if your parents are on a "rag on your friends" campaign, there may be a few hidden reasons why they're saying what they're saying. When you hop in your friend's car and he burns rubber all the way down the street, that tends to wrinkle parents' foreheads. If a girlfriend shows up at the door smelling like a vodka factory, it only takes a whiff for your folks to know she's flammable. If your friend calls on the phone, and your mom asks him where you're going and hears a completely different version from what you just told her, she'll worry. Sometimes your dangerous friends are not too subtle.

If your parents are concerned about your choice of friends, God is even more concerned. God knows how dangerous friends can lead you away from the friendship he wants to share with you. God not only wants you to know him as a

perfect and wonderful friend, but also as a powerful and loving Lord. He knows that your friends will either pull you closer to or farther from him. Jesus Christ, God's only Son, knows what it's like to have dangerous friends. Judas, a dangerous friend who hung out with Jesus for three years, betrayed him for thirty pieces of silver. Are you going to sell out for Jesus or sell out for your friends? Jesus is the wisest friend you could ever choose to have. Walk with Jesus and you'll grow wise. Hanging out with fools only brings you harm, and dangerous friends are fools.

THE STRATEGY

Good friends are sometimes hard to find. Ask yourself these questions:

Who are my real friends?
Do my friends build me up or pull me down?
How do my friends help me grow in my relationship with
　God?
Can I absolutely trust my friends?
What characteristics do I look for in my friends?
Do I pull my friends up or tear them down?

Look up the following verses to discover some of the characteristics of a good friend. After reading each verse, write down what you believe God is saying to you in his Word. Then write down a specific situation that would apply to the message of the verse. What friend of yours demonstrates the characteristics of each verse?

I am a friend to all who fear you,
　to all who follow your precepts.
　　　　Psalm 119:63

A friend loves at all times,
　and a brother is born for adversity.
　　　　Proverbs 17:17

A man of many companions may come to ruin,
　but there is a friend who sticks closer than a brother.
　　　　Proverbs 18:24

Wounds from a friend can be trusted,
　but an enemy multiplies kisses.
　　　　Proverbs 27:6

If one falls down,
　his friend can help him up.

> But pity the man who falls
> and has no one to help him up!
>
> Ecclesiastes 4:10

You adulterous people, don't you know that friendship with the world is hatred toward God? Anyone who chooses to be a friend of the world becomes an enemy of God.

James 4:4

> Do not make friends with a hot-tempered man,
> do not associate with one easily angered.
>
> Proverbs 22:24

Greater love has no one than this, that he lay down his life for his friends. You are my friends if you do what I command. I no longer call you servants, because a servant does not know his master's business. Instead, I have called you friends, for everything that I learned from my Father I have made known to you.

John 15:13–15

18 Premarital Sex

Don't Do "IT!"

THE SITUATION

"What in the world are you two doing?" your Gumby-eyeballed father screams. Your pale-faced mother, hand to mouth, gasps at the sight of you and your girlfriend, tangled octopus fashion, doing an experimental lip-o-suction project on the couch that was definitely not assigned by your anatomy teacher. Sorry, no extra credit for this one.

"NO, NO, Mom and Dad . . . this isn't what you think," you stammer, suddenly creating an explanation for your unexplainable, interactive, extracurricular activity. *Say something quick; Mom's about to pass out!*

In desperation, tears, sweat, panic, and embarrassment, you blurt out, "You see, Julie and I have this CPR class and we were, uh, well, I was practicing mouth-to-mouth recreation . . . NO, NO, I mean, resuscitation." Your girlfriend passes out.

"Mouth-to-mouth resuscitation?!" explodes your unbelieving dad, with thick, purple veins now pulsating on his crimson neck. "Do I look like I just parachuted in from the fifth century? I told you not to do *it!* What do you think I am? Stupid?" *I didn't say it, Dad, you did.*

You thought your parents were going to dinner *and* a movie. Wrong! You didn't hear them pull up. You didn't hear the slam of car doors. The squeaky opening of the front door fell upon your deaf ears. Only when their feet hit the hardwood floor as they turned the corner into the den saying, "Tim, Julie, are you . . ." did a little tiny hand type this All Points Bulletin, Red Alert, nuclear DEFCOM 5 message in your brain 4.8 nanoseconds too late: Y-O-U-'R-E-D-E-A-D-M-E-A-T!!

THE SCRIPTURE

Flee from sexual immorality. All other sins a man commits are outside his body, but he who sins sexually sins against his own body. Do you not know that your body is a temple of the Holy Spirit, who is in you, whom you have received from God? You are not your own; you were bought at a price. Therefore honor God with your body.

1 Corinthians 6:18–20

Don't do what? What does "IT" mean? What're your mom and dad saying when they look at you and say, "You know what I'm talking about!"

*No, Mom, I don't know what you're talking about . . . what are you talking about? I don't respond to your saying "IT" just like you don't respond to my saying "Huh?" Besides, you're also speaking in that adult, roundabout, beat-around-the-proverbial-bush-take-the-fourth-exit-turn-left-and-hope-that-the-word-we're-both-thinking-about-is-the-same-word-everyone-else-calls-*sex *way of speaking. According to basic language usage,* IT *could mean anything from pole-vaulting in the rain with your hands full of Vaseline and no pad to land on, to taking the week off from doing my chores. Is that* IT? *Have I got* IT?

Your folks may have a difficult time talking to you about something someone else probably didn't explain very well to them. Yeah, you got "it," we're talking about sex. What some parents make confusing or simply remain silent about, God speaks loud and clear about. God doesn't just say, "Don't do IT," he gives clear reasons why not. First of all, God says to flee from sexual immorality, because being sexually active outside of marriage messes up your relationship with him. Second, God says that being sexually active before you're married messes up your relationship with yourself. When you sin sexually, you sin against yourself. Whoa! Why? It's because he has placed his Holy Spirit in you, and your body is a temple, a home, a place where he wants to live and dwell. God places a big importance on the body he gave you. That's what he means when he says, "Hey look! You're not your own anymore. You're mine because you've been bought with a price." Honor God with your body by saving yourself for someone you can spend your life with. Don't trade something temporary like sex for someone eternal like God. Get it?

THE STRATEGY

This one's gonna be a stretch for you—a BIG stretch. In fact, I dare you, I double-dog dare you, I triple-dog dare you to write down any three questions about sex, and go ask your parents your questions. Just think what a reaction you'll get from your friends when they ask you on the way to school what you did last night. "Oh, I had three really important questions about sex that I was dying to talk to my folks about. We ended up talking for over an hour. What did you do?"

You may have one question or a million, but if you initiate the conversation with your folks (if they haven't already initiated talking to you about sex), then they'll know you're serious. Maybe there's a good reason why you don't feel comfortable talking to your parents about sex. That's OK too. The important thing is that you talk to someone you respect, someone who's going to give you the facts, and someone who's going to tell you what God thinks about sex. Maybe that someone is a coach, teacher, youth pastor, or family friend. Whomever you bring your questions about sex to, remember you don't have to be afraid of speaking about it. God created IT, and he calls IT sex.

Safe Living

Don't Take the Car—You'll Kill Yourself!

THE SITUATION

A few years ago during Easter vacation, forty high school students and six leaders from the youth group I led went to Mexicali, Mexico, for a week of working with local churches, teenagers, and runny-nosed kids. After spending seven days living in talcum powder-like dust, eating canned food, and sleeping on rock-hard ground, we packed up and headed back to the U.S.

Fifteen minutes after crossing the border, while traveling on a two-lane desert road, our group of vans came upon a motorcycle accident. As we slowly drove by, we saw two women kneeling in the middle of the road, blood all over their hands, hunched over a teenage boy while desperately trying to pump life into him by giving him CPR. We pulled over, and two of our staff, one a paramedic, the other a nurse, attempted to take control of the chaotic scene. With her son's blood all over her face, hands, and soaking her jeans from the knees down, the boy's mother was absolutely hysterical. His father walked around in a dazed, numb state, knowing that his critically injured son probably wouldn't survive. Ryan, thirteen years old, clung to me with a vise grip, screaming and crying for his fifteen-year-old brother, Sean, not to die. For the next forty-five minutes, our staff struggled to save Sean's life.

As we waited for the ambulance to arrive, we found out that the family of four, Mom, Dad, Sean, and Ryan, plus two family friends, were spending the Easter vacation riding motorcycles in the desert. Sean and his dad were ahead of the other four on a dirt road that intersected the highway. Immediately after crossing the highway, Sean turned around to go back to the others. Not looking before he crossed the highway, he didn't see a car rapidly approaching him at 60–70 mph. Sean was hit, launched into the air, and thrown onto the pavement like a rag doll. Struck by a car weighing a thousand pounds more than he, his helmet didn't help much. After the longest forty-five minutes of our lives, the paramedics and police finally arrived. Sean, only fifteen years old, was declared dead.

THE SCRIPTURE

> Now choose life, so that you and your children may live and that you may love the LORD your God, listen to his voice, and hold fast to him. For the LORD is your life. . . .
>
> Deuteronomy 30:19–20

The intense screams of Sean's mother and younger brother shattered the desert's silence, while the students in our vans shuddered as they watched this family begin the painful process of grief. Our leaders cleaned Sean's blood off their hands, and we returned to the vans and drove to a rest stop.

For the next hour, our team of students and leaders cried, prayed together, hugged one another, and shared what we were feeling to try to make sense of what had just happened. A fifteen-year-old guy was gone—dead, his life finished.

Students shared such thoughts as, "That could have been me." "He was just like one of us." "He will never get his driver's license or graduate from high school . . . things I look forward to and take for granted." Sean's death is a grim, graphic reminder of the fine line dividing the two-lane highway of life and death.

Traveling to Mexico for many years on work projects with teenagers, I've had many parents ask me important questions such as, Is it safe to drive in Mexico? Will my son or daughter be OK? How many times have you taken students on long driving trips? What kinds of cars are you driving in? Hearing questions like those, I've been able to make a simple observation: Your parents are concerned about your safety. Whenever you get in a car, they want to be sure that you'll get out safely.

Not only are your parents concerned about your safety, but so is God. When you get behind the wheel of a car or hop in a car loaded with your friends, choosing life means doing all the stuff your folks remind you about: wearing seatbelts, not picking up hitch-hikers, no stunt-car driving or Mario Andretti aspirations. Safe driving is a practical way to choose life so you can experience all the life God has prepared for you.

THE STRATEGY

Think about someone you know who has been injured or was killed in a car accident. Not a very pleasant thought, is it? What were the conditions surrounding the accident? Who was at fault? How could the accident have been avoided? How could safer driving have made a difference?

No one ever thinks, "Oh, I think I'll go get in a car wreck today." Accidents happen when we least expect them. That's why it's critical to make decisions that choose life and not death. Here are a few things to think about when getting into a car:

Are all four wheels on the car?
Who's driving?
Does the car have a spare tire?
What are the road conditions?
Is the car working properly?
Does the driver have insurance?
Has the driver ever been cited for speeding or car accidents?
What kind of reputation as a driver does the person behind the wheel have?
Does the car have airbags?
Does your friend have permission to be driving?
Is the car stolen?

20 — Family Rules

As Long As You're Living under This Roof, You'll Do As I Say!

THE SITUATION

"You are part of this family. If you want to live in this house, then there're going to be some rules around here. If you don't like it here, you can pack up and leave. So, as long as you're living under this roof, you'll do as I say."

Seven silent children sat on the couch, staring, not saying a word. Say one word and you were dead. It was another Family Meeting in progress, and the progress report wasn't very good. We were in trouble. Again.

"Does anyone have anything to say?" my father asked, concluding the same remarks we had heard for years. Any one of us kids could have stood in for him.

Neil spoke first, "I think Dad's right. The girls need to do more work."

"Sit down, Neil, or you'll be pulling weeds for weeks," said my unamused dad.

In tears, Colleen cried, "It's not fair that I'm the oldest and have to do more work than everyone else." Colleen *always* cried at Family Meetings.

Jeers rang out . . .

"Yeah, right! Put a lid on it!" "Get a violin and go cry in a bucket." Six sympathetic siblings.

Kathy, the most reasonable one in the bunch, spoke up and said, "What really needs work around here is Dish Night! There're some people in here who don't do the dishes on their night like they're supposed to."

Voices barked in . . .

"Now wait a minute!" "Like who? Who doesn't do their dishes on Dish Night? Who? Who?"

"Like you, Joey. Whenever it's your turn for the dishes, right after dinner's over you always say, 'I've got to go to the bathroom,' and you stay in there for an hour!"

What can I say? Hiding out in the bathroom got me out of doing dishes.

THE SCRIPTURE

You, my brothers, were called to be free. But do not use your freedom to indulge the sinful nature; rather, serve one another in love.

Galatians 5:13

Seven kids; seven nights in a week; seven dinners in a week: one Dish Night per kid. My parents scored on that planning. Dish Night was a frequent source of tension and administrative agony in our family. If Mom felt like making a big tuna casserole with sides of veggies, bread, salad, and ice cream for dessert, whoever had Dish Night was still washing dishes after everyone else had gone to bed. And then there were the lucky ones who got Dish Night on the weekends. Everyone was out of the house!

Every family has a set of rules. Family Meetings were the times when my dad reminded us what the rules were. My dad would be a millionaire if he had a nickel for every time someone said, "That's a rule?! I've never heard that one before!" Rules were rules, and if you weren't willing to stick by the rules in our house, then you'd better be ready to pull weeds. I think my dad kept a huge bag of weed seed in the garage just to keep us busy.

Taking your family for granted is an easy thing to do because living in a family can give you a lot of freedom. Paul says not to use your freedom to pig out on selfishness. Paul says to serve one another in love (instead of hiding in the bathroom during Dish Night). You can choose to grudgingly go by the rules, which is a drag, or you can choose to serve your family in love. Going by the rules is a notch above mere existence, but serving your family in love is living on the edge for God. You can sneak away or serve up a lifestyle of love. Be forewarned: If you sneak away, all those missed Dish Nights will soon catch up with you. I now do the dishes almost every night–just ask my wife!

THE STRATEGY

How do you try to get out of chores in your home? What rules are you most likely to break? How do you avoid doing what you know your folks expect you to do? Take a few minutes to evaluate how you serve your family. What makes it difficult for you to serve them? How can you improve in loving and serving them? How could things be better in your home by your helping out? Could you be convicted in a court of law for serving your family in love? Write down two specific ways you can serve your family this week and pray for God to give you the desire and strength to do so.

Call If You're Going to Be Late!

THE SITUATION

"Hello, is this Joey?"

Grunt. Groan. Sniff. Sniff. Scratch. Shake head. Clear throat. Rub eyelids.

"Yeah, who's this? How can I help you?" At one o'clock in the morning?

"This is Mrs. Don't-Know-Where-My-Kid-Is. I'm sorry I'm calling so late, but I wanted to know if my son showed up at your youth group event tonight. It's almost one in the morning and he's not home yet. Do you know where he and the other people he was with might be?"

Do I know where they might be? Do I have the cure for bad breath? Do I know the temperature of the sun? Do I know how many little black and white penguins are in Antarctica? Do I know the country code to phone Pakistan?

Oh yes, I believe I can locate your son . . . just let me check my Lost-Son-Scanner Monitor right here next to my bed . . . OK, I've located him. My gauges are reading that right now he's traveling in a late model, four-door sedan, color pea green, at thirty-eight miles per hour on State Street, heading north/northwest, and will arrive at John Smith's home in approximately 3.2 minutes. There are four occupants in the car, two male, two female; male Caucasian driving, age estimated is 16.5 years old, one point on driving record. Would you like the phone number of John Smith's home? I can bring it up on the screen, but of course, you'd have to wake up two households in one night.

Do I know where your son is at one o'clock in the morning? I've only received a few late-night phone calls from panicky parents over the years, but that's been enough for me to want to strangle their son or daughter the following week. Every student in our youth ministry quickly learned to call home if they were going to be late. It only takes one or two examples to motivate the others to action.

THE SCRIPTURE

Each of you should look not only to your own interests, but also to the interests of others.

Philippians 2:4

It happens all the time. You decide to get pizza after practice with some of your teammates. You decide you want to pump weights just twenty minutes longer. Your breakup with your boyfriend is taking much longer than you expected. There are all sorts of reasons that you don't make it home at the time you told your parents. So, you know what sometimes happens when you don't call: Your parents think the worst. *My son has been killed or seriously injured in a car accident. My daughter has been kidnapped. My precious child is alone, helpless without me to save her!*

Kind of extreme? Yeah, but it doesn't take many nights of watching the news, *Hard Copy*, *Rescue 911*, and *The Highway Patrol* for your parents' imaginations to run wild like an out-of-control freight train. Even E.T. knew how to phone home. If a little, sun-wrinkled raisin of an alien can phone home, your parents expect that you can at least do the same.

Calling your parents if you're going to be late is a simple way of considering their interests before your own. Most of the time, your parents will be flexible when you show you've been responsible and considerate. If you're not able to keep your commitment about when you said you'd be home, calling home at least gives your parents the chance to know where you are and what time you will be home. Then they can watch *Rescue 911* in peace.

Jesus was always looking out for the interests of others. He was considerate of others' feelings and fears. By calling home, you show your parents that you care about their feelings and their fears. Even if it's late, even one o'clock in the morning, your parents would rather speak to you than wake up your youth pastor. I hope.

THE STRATEGY

Tape two quarters to your forehead, waist belt, wallet, purse, dashboard, or on the engine block. If you're going to be late, call home. If in doubt, call home. If you're scared to wake up your parents, wake 'em up anyway. That way your youth pastor will have a good night's sleep!

You'd Better Watch the Tone of Your Voice, Young Lady!

THE SITUATION

There have been a number of parents of students in our youth ministry over the years who haven't been very worthy of their son's or daughter's respect. Yep, you heard me right. Some parents are not worthy!

I'm not talking about the type of dad who collars your boyfriend the moment he walks through the front door, grabs a stack of dusty family photo albums, and embarrasses you to death by showing your boyfriend baby photos of you doing the backstroke in the bathtub. For that type of minor offense, you have the right to go into your dad's car and crank up the radio volume so he gets a sonic concussion when he starts the car tomorrow morning.

When I say some parents aren't worthy of respect, I'm thinking of the extreme—the more serious situations I've experienced the past few years.

- Parents who smoke pot and tell their kids not to use drugs
- Parents who sexually molest or physically abuse their children
- Parents who sponsor kegger parties
- Moms and dads who use the Bible like a whip to justify their own manipulative behaviors
- Parents who deny that their son or daughter has a drinking problem

These parents are on the far side of the Bell Curve. They don't fall in the normal range. They're extreme. Unreasonable. Malicious. Unfair. And in some cases, very sick individuals. They're the type of parents who deserve and receive very little respect. Perhaps you live with one?

THE SCRIPTURE

> The tongue also is a fire, a world of evil among the parts of the body. It corrupts the whole person, sets the whole course of his life on fire, and is itself set on fire by hell.
>
> All kinds of animals, birds, reptiles and creatures of the sea are being tamed and have been tamed by man, but no man can tame the tongue. It is a restless evil, full of deadly poison.
>
> James 3:6–8

If you live in a situation like I just described, then my encouragement to you is to get help. Talk to an adult you can trust—a youth pastor, a teacher, or a coach who will listen to you. Serious problems tend to switch people into survival mode, but your best chances of surviving a negative home life is getting the help you need. Your home life goes far beyond the respect issue we're talking about in this chapter. Don't wait. Let others help you. Get help today.

If you're not in the group I just described (and I hope you're not!), one of the simplest ways to show respect to your parents is to watch your words. Watching your words and the tone of your voice shows and earns respect from your parents.

When the tone of your voice goes from peaceful to defensive and accusatory, depending on how your parents handle verbal assaults, your words can act like a shovel to dig your own grave. That's why parents quickly send up warning flares for you to watch the tone of your voice.

If there is one muscle group that you want to work on as a Christian, then work on the tongue muscle. The Bible says that the tongue is one of the most powerful forces known to mankind. The tongue is capable of breaking hearts, crushing spirits, and destroying dreams. The bitter, harmful words we say not only destroy everything in their path, but eventually come back to burn us too. When was the last time your words torched someone you really love? That little wet piece of muscle is stronger than any beast, and by man's own strength is impossible to tame.

God is the only one who can give you the strength to tame your tongue. The Holy Spirit can give you the wisdom and strength to watch your words rather than hurt others. The Holy Spirit can give you patience, self-control, and peace when you feel like lashing your tongue like a whip. Instead of giving your parents a bitter cup of deadly poison to drink with your words, you, by God's Spirit, can use your words to encourage and refresh them. Watch your words . . . that'll earn your parents' respect.

THE STRATEGY

Carry around a mini-cassette recorder or small tape recorder. You may need to borrow one from your mom or dad. Tape the conversations you have with your friends. Tape the conversations you have with your brothers and sisters. To be really daring, tape your conversations with your parents. Go back and listen to the words you use and the tone of your voice. What did you notice? Whom do you watch your words with? What people are you nicest to? What did you sound like when you were talking to your parents? Did you notice any difference between when you speak to your friends and when you speak to your family?

23 Pushing
the Limit

Do That One More Time and Your Name Is Mud!

THE SITUATION

"Stop touching me!"

"I'm not touching you!"

"Get your hand out of my face!"

"Don't touch my hand. I can put it here if I want to. I'm not touching you!"

I used to be really good at irritating my sisters. Holding my hand two inches from their face, I'd follow them around, not touching them, but just keeping my hand right where they could see it. I had a right to put my hand in the air, didn't I?

The TV channel changer was also a source of major irritation. In our house, the channel changer was appropriately called "the dictator." Whoever had the dictator ruled every program and station. My brother and I liked to watch Bruce

Lee, Godzilla, Rodan, and Giant Robot movies during the afternoon. That was about the same time my sister's favorite soap operas came on. I can still remember my sister impatiently saying, "OK, it's a commercial now, switch it to General Hospital."

Irritating my sisters was one thing. I could push their limit as far as I wanted to have their fingernails dug into my arm. But my parents had a lower level of irritation tolerance. Neil and I, members of Future Gardeners of America, had to work in the yard helping my dad rake, hoe, cut, plant, and hose down. After hours of horticultural boredom, one of us would eventually start a water fight, dirt fight, weed fight, ice plant fight, or hoe fight. Accidentally, my dad would get a dousing of water or a dirt clod in the back. You know what would happen if Neil and I did that one more time.

THE SCRIPTURE

> He lifted me out of the slimy pit,
>   out of the mud and mire;
> he set my feet on a rock
>   and gave me a firm place to stand.
> Psalm 40:2

The teenage years are those in-between years when you're not considered a child anymore, but nobody is actually ready to call you an adult. So what do you do to find out where you stand? You push the limit. Why? Because the old limits of being a little kid are gone. Let's hope your mom doesn't bathe and dress you anymore. And she probably doesn't tuck you in and read the Berenstain Bears. You're probably not eighteen yet either, out on your own, in college or working full-time, paying the rent, scraping up money for car payments and bills, doing whatever you want with your time. Adulthood hasn't arrived, so you're left waiting in junior high and high school.

Pushing the limit has its benefits because you're in the critical process of establishing your own identity. You are discovering your strengths and weaknesses, your personality when you're alone and with other people. That's important for discovering who you are, but not at the cost of irritating others. Pushing the limit by driving your parents crazy or making poor decisions that can harm others or yourself is what will motivate your parents to change your name on your birth certificate to "Mud."

God doesn't want your name to be mud for pushing the limit. He wants you to stand firm in your faith in Jesus Christ. Irritating others and thinking only of yourself are negative actions that stunt your growth in God. As you begin to discover who you are as a Christian, a person who is fearfully and wonderfully made by God, one of the first things you'll want to do is to allow God to set your feet on the foundation of his Word. God will make your steps solid as you move out of the mud and into the process of maturing in Christ. Don't worry, you won't be alone. Jesus Christ is the one who will walk with you all the way.

THE STRATEGY

Instead of irritating your little brother or sister like I did, why not think of some ways to help them out? How can you give your parents a hand this week in the house or in the yard? It's OK to have fun with your family, but knowing when to cool it by balancing your craziness with service will show them that you really care.

On the next page there's an idea for a coupon book that you can give to your family. It's loaded with offers that will please rather than irritate them.

FAMILY COUPON BOOK

GOOD FOR:

- ❖ 1 free car wash
- ❖ 1 free back rub
- ❖ 1 free dish night
- ❖ 1 free take out trash
- ❖ 1 free room cleaning
- ❖ 1 free family room cleaning
- ❖ 1 free hour of typing

- ❖ 1 free dinner
- ❖ 1 free hour of yard work
- ❖ 1 free night of baby-sitting
- ❖ 1 free clean out refrigerator
- ❖ 1 free garage cleanout
- ❖ 1 free hour of tutoring
- ❖ 1 free dusting & vacuuming

COUPON

GOOD FOR:

1 FREE CAR WASH

24 Regret

You'll Be Sorry!

THE SITUATION

In eighth grade, I thought I was cool—really cool. I was on one of the top skateboarding teams in the country. I traveled all over California for competitions and demonstrations. I received tons of skateboards, clothes, and equipment. I even made skateboarding history by being the first skateboarder to perform on *Romper Room*. Needless to say, on and off campus, I thought I was better than your average Joe.

My sister Loretta was a year younger than I, and she attended the same private school I used to attend. Fortunately, my parents allowed me to go to Niguel Hills Junior High for eighth grade. Going from a private to a public school made me cooler than a walk-in refrigerator on a hot summer day. Like most eighth grade guys, I was definitely cooler than my younger sister.

The upcoming dance on Friday night at Niguel Hills was going to be cool. I was going to the dance with all my cool friends to dance with cool girls. Our next door neighbor, Patty, invited Loretta to go to the dance with her. That was not cool. Loretta was invading my cool territory.

I told Patty that if she wanted to be my friend, she had to tell Loretta she wasn't able to get her a ticket. Patty protested, "What's the big deal? It's just a dance . . . why can't she go?" Patty didn't understand. I told Patty that she was not being cool. I reminded her that it wasn't cool for me to have my uncool little sister at a cool dance. Patty gave in to me. Cool.

The dance was cool. Loretta wasn't able to make it because Patty failed to get her a ticket. When I got home that night, the rest of my sisters were calling Patty all sorts of names. Things were not looking cool; they were heating up.

Earlier that day, my mom took Loretta to have her hair cut and bought her a new dress for the dance. This was Loretta's first dance, and my mom said she had never seen Loretta so excited. They arrived home with the new dress and haircut. Loretta was ready to have the best night of her life—until Patty came over.

THE SCRIPTURE

> Godly sorrow brings repentance that leads to salvation and leaves no regret, but worldly sorrow brings death.
>
> 2 Corinthians 7:10

What I did to Loretta was not cool. In the name of cool, I crushed her with self-centeredness and conceit. My sisters told me that when Loretta found out there wasn't a ticket for her for the dance, she cried on her bed for an hour. I remember my mom saying, "I'm so mad at Patty! How could she forget to get her a dance ticket when she's the one who invited her to go?" I said nothing.

A couple days went by, and my coolness turned into crud. I felt awful. I had a hollow, nauseous feeling in the pit of my stomach. I had blown it in a major way. Loretta had done nothing to me, and for no reason other than being cool, I had put myself before my sister. When I realized how much I had hurt her, I really regretted living for myself and for cool.

On the following Sunday afternoon, Loretta and I went to the mall. All afternoon long I waited and stalled for the chance to tell her the truth. Standing next to the second-story railing right outside Bullocks Department Store, I told Loretta the real reason why Patty had failed to get her a ticket. I told her that I was a complete jerk, that I was really sorry; and I asked for her forgiveness. Loretta forgave me. *That was cool.*

Parents issue "You'll be sorry" threats all the time. Now I know why. When we spend our lives just thinking of ourselves, eventually we will be sorry. Seeing how the pain we inflict on others destroys their spirit, that same pain boomerangs back and destroys our spirit as well.

Do you want to live with regret or salvation? The Bible says that godly sorrow brings repentance which leads to salvation. Sorrow for sorrow's sake brings nothing but death. You and I have the choice to live a life of repentance (turning away from sin) or a life of regret. Living with regret is a sure way to waste your life. Don't be too cool to say you're sorry.

THE STRATEGY

Whom have you hurt recently? Have you said or done anything that crushed someone else? It takes a lot of guts to admit you're wrong. It takes even more to ask for forgiveness. Maybe there's someone who has really hurt you. Maybe you've been the target of someone's attack and have been wounded by harsh words. Forgiving someone else is just as courageous as asking for forgiveness. The action step for today is simple: Whether you've been hurt or done the hurting, ask God for the courage to mend a broken relationship. He will give you his grace and strength to give and receive forgiveness.

Stop Your Crying or I'll Really Give You Something to Cry About!

THE SITUATION

"This is lame."

"I never get to do anything."

"Tom's parents let him do anything he wants."

"This sucks."

"This is rank."

"How come you only treat me this way?"

"I can't wait until I'm eighteen."

"We've been waiting for hours . . . when are we going to leave?"

"I'm never going to treat my kids like you treat me!"

"This food is disgusting."

"Dad, you OWE me my allowance."

"Is that all the money I get?"

"I hate you with all I have in me."
"I want to go live with Mom."
"I'm sick of this house."
"Why won't you let me do what my friends' parents let them do?"
"You don't trust me."
"You always treat me like a little kid."

How would you feel if you were battle-rammed with negative, whining, poisonous comments like this on a regular basis? Chances are, your parents don't spank you anymore or never did, but enough comments like these may cause them to reconsider it. If you've ever baby-sat a kid who screamed at glass-breaking decibels for two hours because Mommy and Daddy left him, you can appreciate the desperation in the stomach-acid-producing words, "Stop your crying or I'll really give you something to cry about!"

THE SCRIPTURE

Do everything without complaining or arguing.
Philippians 2:14

As a kid, you did your fair share of crying. A beheaded Barbie doll; a fight on the playground; maybe even getting teased on the bus home from school—crying was a part of growing up. As teenagers, however, complaining, pouting, manipulating, arguing, and whining have replaced the more simple and effective act of shedding a tear or two. Of course, it's not real cool to cry (especially if you're a guy), and it looks real cool to your friends if you stand up to your parents. But then again, you have to live with your folks and not your friends.

God knows that complaining and arguing drive parents crazy. When was the last time complaining drove you crazy? I used to be on a volleyball team with a guy whose sole purpose in life was to blame others for any and everything, cuss about this, and complain about that. He never, I mean never, had one good thing to say about anything. He was a real fun guy to be around. A big baby!

God wants to help you move from being part of the problem to part of the solution. That's the difference between a teenager who's growing in his or her faith and a teenager who's stuck in the sin of badattituditis. Doing everything without complaining or arguing will prevent your folks from really giving you something to cry about.

THE STRATEGY

Take a few minutes to look up the following verses about attitudes. Rewrite the verses in your own words. Now write down how the verse relates to your life. Think of a step you can take to begin living with the kind of attitude God wants you to have.

1 Peter 4:1–2

_____

_____

Philippians 2:4–8

_____

_____

Ephesians 4:22–24

_____

_____

Hebrews 4:12

_____

_____

26 Parenting

Just Wait Until You're a Parent Someday!

THE SITUATION

What could be so difficult about raising seven kids? What is so hard about trying to feed, burp, bathe, change, and put to bed seven kids born in eight years? What could be so hard about teaching, correcting, understanding, and deciphering language skills that range from "Goo-goo-gaw-gaw" to "Gimme my granola bar!"?

There was the time when my mom made a "wonderful" new recipe for Swedish meatballs. My dad was planning on taking all seven kids to my cousin Kenny's basketball game, so we wolfed down the wonderful Swedish meatballs in a hurry and headed to the game. (I personally thought they tasted like Science Diet Dogfood.) Before the game reached halftime, half the O'Connor kids were painting the bleachers with meatball shakes. My mother had poisoned us all!

Then there was the time when my dad drove us from Los Angeles to Arizona, across the baking desert, in the middle of August. Nine of us were packed in our red Country Squire with the fake wood on the side and luggage on top. The whole way to Arizona, Loretta kept complaining about her back itching.

"Colleen, scratch my back. Scratch my back, it itches!"

We arrived in Arizona to chase lizards, count rocks, and stay away from Loretta. She had chicken pox!

Then there was the time when my sister Kathy was a toddler and decided to do what toddlers do best: frighten their parents. Naked as a jaybird, she toddled right outside the second-story window and onto the red-tile roof. Toddling around the tile roof, she waved to my parents twenty feet below. Rushing to rescue her before she toppled off, my dad grabbed Kathy and brought her safely inside where he could put some clothes on her.

THE SCRIPTURE

> Children's children are a crown to the aged,
> and parents are the pride of their children.
>   Proverbs 17:6

Now I know. Now I know what my parents were talking about every time they said to us, "Just you wait and see. Just wait until you're a parent someday." Now I'm a dad with a beautiful wife, a wild, fun four-year-old daughter, and a smiling four-month-old baby girl. Now I know how hard it can be raising two children, let alone seven. I don't see how my parents were able to accomplish such a feat. My mom says she just blocked it all out.

Being a parent isn't easy. Just as you face all sorts of difficult decisions to make about your life, so do your parents about their lives.

I'm not your parent. But I am a parent, and I know now that the things I said to my parents as a teenager weren't always the best or the coolest. At one time or another, in a rage of emotion and anger, I think each of us kids said to my parents, "When I grow up and have my own kids, I'm never going to raise them like you've raised me!" My parents took comments like that in perspective knowing that *someday* we'd be parents too.

Because my parents hung in there with me, never giving up on me and always believing in me, this Bible verse now makes a lot of sense to me. *Parents are the pride of their children.* I wasn't very thankful as a teenager, but I sure am grateful now for the parents God gave me. Even if your parents have hurt you in a very powerful way, you still have a parent in heaven who loves and cares about you. You have a heavenly Father who loves and believes in you. If you have great parents, thank God and thank your parents. If your mom or dad aren't the best around, don't give up on God, and don't give up on them. They're the only ones you have.

THE STRATEGY

Surprise your parents by writing them a letter telling them how you feel. Thank them for the specific ways they have helped you over the years. Think of funny memories you've shared, tough times you've made it through, and the moments you remember the best. Tell them the special characteristics you see in both their lives and how those have made a difference in your life. Write down a favorite Bible verse that reminds you of them. Ask your parents out to dinner on you!

27   Honoring

You'll Do It in My Time, Not Yours!

THE SITUATION

It's Friday afternoon and school's finally out for the week. Before you take off with your friends tonight, you decide to spend the late afternoon kicking back in front of the TV, eating Doritos and drinking Coke, watching your favorite music videos. You hear your dad's car pull up and think to yourself, "That's funny. Dad doesn't usually get home this early." Just then, something clicks in your brain. You remember your yard work isn't finished.

"I've got a lot of things I want you to do this week. I know it's more work than usual, but we've got to get this house clean for the party on Saturday night. I want you to . . .

    mow the lawn
    cut the hedge
    trim the grass
    pull weeds

pull out the dead flowers
plant new ones
fertilize the planters
fix the broken sprinkler heads
paint the gazebo
clean the pool
rake the leaves
hose the patio
clean the patio furniture
then come see me when you're done

You accomplished a few things earlier in the week like buying the fertilizer and hosing down the patio, but you are still a long way from being done. Didn't your dad realize how much homework you had this week? And didn't he know that you'd already promised your friends you'd play baseball with them?

Your dad walks in the door, and you can already tell by the look on his face that he's not a happy camper. You know now you're in big trouble. Music blaring from the TV, you look up and faintly smile, "Hi, Dad! Want a Dorito?"

THE SCRIPTURE

"Honor your father and mother"—which is the first commandment with a promise—"that it may go well with you and that you may enjoy long life on the earth."

Ephesians 6:2–3

Parents aren't too difficult to please. Sure, some parents have a list of unrealistic expectations as high as the World Trade Center, but that's not true of all parents. In fact, God's command to honor your father and mother is something that he believes you can do. What makes it hard to honor your mom and dad? Why is it difficult to do things in their time instead of your own time?

As a teenager, I tended to complicate things. My dad would ask me to clean the garage, and I'd try to connive my way out of it or put it off until later. The more I resisted, the more upset he got. I turned a simple twenty-minute job into a heated debate and ordeal. I made life difficult for myself—and for my dad.

Avoiding chores is a common way of creating unnecessary chaos for everyone. Why make life harder on yourself and your parents when you can develop your parents' trust? Remember, if you can be trusted with little responsibilities, then you'll probably be trusted with greater responsibilities, especially in the things you want to do.

God says to honor your parents that it may go well with you. He wants you to enjoy a long life, and he wants your parents to enjoy a long life. In order to enjoy life instead of strife, you need to be willing to follow your parents' wishes. When you honor your parents, you honor God by showing him you're serious about his commands for you. You're saying to God, "God, I'm going to do things your way and not my way, in your time and not my time."

THE STRATEGY

There are all sorts of ways to honor your parents. Write down the things you've been doing in your own time instead of your parents' time. What do you need to do to change? Do you and your folks need to talk about how much work you do? Do you need to schedule your time better? How can your parents help you out in this area? Ask God to help you honor him by honoring your parents. He will give you all of his time to help you do things in your parents' time.

Profanity

You Will Never Say That Word Again in This House! . . . Do You Understand Me?

THE SITUATION

Do you ever feel a little daring? Do you ever feel like you want to show your parents how much you really know? Have you ever had the urge to demonstrate your knowledge of the world through your expanding vocabulary?

It doesn't take much to make your mom or dad mad. In fact, all it takes are a few choice, carefully selected, USDA prime-cut words straight out of the sewer and you'll have your parents boiling in seconds. Parents get ticked off with words like !#@*☆ and @◐※⊗#!!*.

Perhaps your friends inspired you with so much bravado. After spending some time at your friends' houses and noticing how freely they use colorful adjectives without incurring the wrath of their parents, you figure that an adjective of your own here and there won't cause much of a stir.

You figure your parents are accomplished, mature adults capable of understanding your worldly wisdom. You theorize that a cuss word, a simple word that expresses dissatisfaction, anger, rage, malice, or slander, is a word your parents have certainly heard before. You also postulate that a cuss word shows how in touch you are, not only with your own generation, but with your parents' generation as well! Doesn't it make good sense for you to bridge the generation gap by spouting off words uttered by your ancestors? Something inside you says, *Go ahead! How could my parents resist such an opportune moment to bond with me, their growing teenager? I can say anything I want. . . .*

"You will never say that word again in this house! . . . Do you understand me?" I didn't say it, your parents did.

THE SCRIPTURE

> When words are many, sin is not absent,
> but he who holds his tongue is wise.
> Proverbs 10:19

It's easy to think that the words our friends use in their houses are the same words you can use in your house. The words you use with your friends and parents serve as good indicators of how much you value them. Your words also show your maturity in Christ or reveal how much more you have to grow. Your parents are trying to develop a certain level of maturity in you before you leave home after high school. That's why your parents may place a very high value on the words you use.

God is also someone who places a big value on the words you choose to use. Why? Because he knows that each one of us is capable of saying words that hurt others. Not only are cuss words on his list of least favorite words, but so are gossiping words, lying words, and slanderous words. Two out of the ten commandments God handed to Moses deal with how we use our tongues (see Deuteronomy 5).

God knows that when we have the tendency to talk a lot, we also have the tendency to sin a lot. Our tongue is like a slippery, wet fish that's hard to hang on to. That's why God says that whoever knows how to hold his or her tongue is wise. Jesus would rather see you fishing for the hearts of other people than always having to fish after a tongue that keeps slipping away. His patience can give you the strength to choose your words wisely. Jesus will keep holding your heart while you keep holding your tongue.

THE STRATEGY

Instead of using words that tear down others, you can use words that build them up. Write down the names of people in your life whom you can help with your words. Here are some creative ways you can make a radical difference in people's lives with the words you use.

Affirmation: Today I will tell John the positive qualities I see in him.

Thankfulness: Today I'll thank my older sister for helping me with homework last night.

Encouragement: Today I'll encourage Sue, who's frustrated about her grades.

Prayer: Today I'm going to let Doug know that I've been praying for his family.

Praise: Today I'm going to praise Jim for all the time he has spent helping others.

29 Thankfulness

Eat Your Dinner. . . . There Are Starving Kids in the World!

THE SITUATION

Around the dinner table at our house, eating a nightly meal was an explosive recipe consisting of seven parts hysteria (one for each kid), three parts whining about what was being served, a dash of excitement for dessert, and two gulps of milk for every one forkful of peas. With seven mouths yapping, the meat was cut and deals were made in order to make us clean our plates. Each child had a unique stealth strategy to lose his or her food without loss of life or going hungry.

My little brother, Neil, was the holy one. My mother pleaded with him, his hands folded and head bowed over his plate, to eat his dinner. Lifting his head, Neil solemnly said, "I'm praying." Twenty minutes later. "Neil, eat your dinner." Neil again lifted his head. "I'm praying."

A few of my sisters had their own thing going, a "girls only" system. Rosemary hid her food in her napkin. Loretta kept the dog well fed. Kathy had an inter-room transport system: food in pocket, excused from table to go to bathroom, dump toxic waste in toilet. Flush. Send the tuna back to sea!

Me? I was stupid. Never, I repeat, never try to sink spinach in milk. First of all, spinach is dark, dark green and does not stay well hidden in a white, watery substance through clear glass. Second, spinach floats. I got nailed for that one and never did it again. With my sisters teaming up on their own and my brother preparing for the monastery, I resorted to gulping down my string beans, meat loaf, peas, broccoli, hamburger helper, and eggplant pizza with gallons of milk. My greatest fear at the dinner table? No more milk.

THE SCRIPTURE

> Give thanks in all circumstances, for this is God's will for you in Christ Jesus.
>
> 1 Thessalonians 5:18

You've heard it a million times, I've heard it a million times: "Eat your dinner . . . there are starving kids in the world!" You've seen the pictures of starving children on TV, I've seen the pictures of starving children on TV. But TV may never change your eating habits or your heart. A starving little child sitting in your lap will.

A few years ago I was in Mexicali, Mexico, for an annual week-long mission outreach with our youth ministry. One morning I was meeting with a few of our student leaders. A little Mexican boy stood nearby while we talked and drank hot chocolate to burn off the morning chill. No more than five or six years old, dirt covering his face, no shoes covering his feet, the little boy clowned around trying to get our attention. We laughed as we watched him, and surprisingly, he mustered up the boldness to plop himself down right in my lap. Seeing we had finished our hot chocolate, one at a time he picked up our cups and began to drink the leftovers. *When was the last time you drank leftover chocolate syrup from the bottom of someone else's cup?*

Giving thanks in all circumstances doesn't mean you have to like what's being served. It's looking past the chipped creamed beef on your plate and realizing that out of all teenagers in the world, you're eating dinner and others are not. It's giving God an honest "thanks" for the clothes in your closet, the roof over your head, the stuff in your room. It's living with a heart that celebrates Thanksgiving every day. Why is it God's will for you to be thankful in all circumstances? A little Mexican kid with chocolate syrup can tell you. He is a real-life reminder of what Mom and Dad have been saying all along.

THE STRATEGY

Take a piece of paper and draw a line down the center of the page. In the left-hand column, write down every material thing you own and are thankful for. For example: chipped creamed beef, CD stereo/cassette player, car, gas in your car so you can go to work to pay for your car, clothes, bed, computer, snowboard, this book, makeup, etc. Now in the right-hand column, write down who gave you everything you own. Maybe you made purchases of your own, maybe other things were gifts, but however you acquired all your stuff, write it down. Now ask yourself the question, "What do I have that other people in the world don't have?"

I hope you'll discover two things: (1) A lot of things you own are, perhaps, gifts from other people. (2) You own a lot more stuff than most people in the world. Take some time to talk with God, telling him thanks for everything you've received and asking him to help you give thanks in all things.

Do I Look Like I'm Made Out of Money?

THE SITUATION

Hey Dad, I need a few bucks for . . .

team uniforms
a Walkman
a new car
pizza
a new bungee cord
lunch
lunch and dinner
501's
a new pair of skis
rollerblades
miniature golf
the car wash
video games

the movies
a date I have with Susan
a CD player
gas
a Cowboys T-shirt
deodorant
a new dress
a ski trip
this book
cowboy boots
a tennis lesson
stable fees
a new muffler

yogurt	*car insurance*
the football game	*a wallet*
the dance	*an L.A. Kings hat*
sunglasses	*a haircut*
a new pair of Nike's	*a cheerleading uniform*

Multiply this list by seven clutching, grabbing, groping pairs of hands and you begin to sense the insanity my dad faced every payday. Isn't one of Dad's duties to dish out cash? Facing a bank line of O'Connor customers waiting to make withdrawals on his wallet, the only thing he could say was, "Do I look like I'm made out of money?"

No, Dad, but the stuff in your wallet will do just fine.

THE SCRIPTURE

> For the love of money is a root of all kinds of evil. Some people, eager for money, have wandered from the faith and pierced themselves with many griefs.
>
> But you, man of God, flee from all this, and pursue righteousness, godliness, faith, love, endurance and gentleness.
>
> 1 Timothy 6:10–11

Your parents aren't made out of money any more than ATMs are made out of human flesh. If you're always asking your mom or dad for money for every single need and desire that you have, they will soon tire of your withdrawals and put a stop payment on your personal account with them.

Why do parents sometimes get tight with money? There are a number of good reasons, some of which can help you become more resourceful with the money you have. First, your mom or dad or both work hard to earn money, which pays for things that teenagers don't always realize cost money. The water in your shower costs money. It costs money to heat the water in your shower. It costs money every time you pick up the phone to call your friends or flip on the light

switch in your room. Nothing is free in this world, and some-one has to pay for it. That's where your parents come in.

Second, your parents have to budget their money. If they don't pay the mortgage, then you may be sleeping in the park across the street. Or if your car insurance or registration fee isn't paid, you won't have a ride to school. (No problem there!) Stuff like food, college funds, medical insurance, and saving money in case of an emergency may be bigger pri-orities to your parents than the latest pair of loose fit, ripped jeans that cost a hundred bucks and will be out of style next month. You decide; do you want to eat or wear the jeans?

Third, if your parents are not always eager to foot the bill every time you need a new pair of Reeboks, it may be because they want you to experience the important reality of earning your own cash. Doing odd jobs, getting a part-time job, or starting your own small business are a few ways to pay for things you may want but your parents can't afford as quickly as you'd like. Earning your own money teaches you how to make important financial decisions that your parents have spent most of their life making for you.

Last, God's Word is filled with mounds of wisdom about the moola in your pocket. The apostle Paul tells us not to be eager to get rich, because focusing too much on money and material things can take our focus off God. Paul even says that a lot of people cash in their relationship with God for money they can see and feel and spend. Don't mortgage your walk with Jesus Christ, especially when he's the one who counted the cost to go to the cross for your sins. Pursue the character of God-like righteousness, godliness, faith, love, endurance, and gentleness. That's a character you'll never lose or get repossessed.

THE STRATEGY

Learning how to use your finances can be a great way to better understand the financial pressure your folks may face. Ask your parents how to do a budget. Look over the monthly bills to see how much money is spent just to keep food in the fridge and a roof over your head. Ask your folks about the investments they make and how they used their money early in their marriage. There are also a lot of good books about financial planning that are easy to read. Be sure to pick up *How to Become a Teenage Millionaire* by Todd Temple (published by Oliver/Nelson). This is a great book, written for teenagers, about how to get, save, spend, and invest your hard-earned cash. Did you know that there are more verses in the Bible that talk about money than there are verses about

God's love, eternity, and heaven? Check out some of these verses to see what God has to say about how to use your money in a way that honors him.

Proverbs 13:11; 17:16   Hebrews 13:5
1 Peter 5:2   Ecclesiastes 5:10; 7:12
Matthew 6:24; 25:14–30   Acts 5:1–10

31 Patience

I'll Be Right Back!

THE SITUATION

Unlike some little kids, my brother, sisters, and I were never in danger of getting kidnapped and held for ransom. Kidnappers avoided our red Country Squire station wagon with the fake wood on the side like they avoided getting hit by a train.

After picking us up from school on weekdays, my mom drove to the Smith Food King. Pulling in front of the store, she always, *always,* said, "I just need to get a couple of things. I'll be right back."

Despite shouts and screams of, "I wanna go in too!" "Can I come in?" "Can I, can I, can I?" "How come Colleen always gets to go in? That's not fair!" my mom told us to stay in the car and be quiet. What happened to the remaining six kids in the car? Oh, nothing but . . . heatstroke because of rolled up windows . . . pinching . . . poking . . . fighting over the radio station . . . old ladies walking by in horror . . . fingers shut in the car door . . . threats of "I'm telling" . . . slapping . . . at least two kids, ten minutes apart, running into the store in tears to find Mom . . . pencils and books flying . . . sighs and cries of "Why is she taking so long? Where is she?"

Forty-five minutes and four overflowing shopping carts later, my mom, Colleen, and two bagboys straining behind the weight of the shopping carts came out with enough food for 2.4 days. "Where have you been," we all cried. "You said you were just going in for a couple things!"

Pulling out a box of ice cream drumsticks, my mom would divert our attention by addressing our starving stomachs instead of our inquiring minds. My mom knew that the key to raising children is the art of distraction.

THE SCRIPTURE

> But for that very reason I was shown mercy so that in me, the worst of sinners, Christ Jesus might display his unlimited patience as an example for those who would believe on him and receive eternal life.
>
> 1 Timothy 1:16

I don't think my mother was trying to teach us patience when she went into the supermarket. She was just trying to buy enough food to keep us from complaining that there was no food in the fridge (but that's a whole other lesson). Patience is a lesson that no one else can teach you. Patience is a lesson that you learn by yourself. You are the teacher and you are the student.

Your parents may tell you that they'll be right back when they step into a store or drop by a friend's house to pick up something, but if you become impatient, it's not because your mom hasn't come right back. Nobody, no thing, or no situation makes us impatient. You choose whether to be patient or not. Patience comes from making the decision to wait and relax.

The other day I was in McDonald's and ordered a McChicken sandwich, a Filet-O-Fish, and a Diet Coke. The

McChicken sandwich and Diet Coke came in a flash, but the Filet-O-Fish hadn't even got off the boat. Five minutes passed. Then ten minutes passed. "Excuse me, ma'am. I ordered a Filet-O-Fish . . . can you tell me what's taking so long?" I was choosing to be impatient. "Filet-O-Fish! Filet-O-Fish," the lady screamed, "put in a Filet-O-Fish!" They hadn't even put it in the hot grease yet!

We need to be merciful to one another. We need each other's patience. Paul says that Jesus showed him, the worst of sinners, unlimited patience as an example so that others would believe in Jesus. Jesus doesn't have to be patient, but in his mercy and love, he chooses to be patient with us so that we can experience a personal and intimate relationship with him.

THE STRATEGY

What situations or problems test your patience the most? What circumstances drive you crazy and make you want to lash out at others? Take a piece of paper and write out all the ways that Jesus shows his unlimited patience with you. How does Jesus want to use your life as an example so that others would believe in him and receive eternal life? How can you tell someone else how Jesus has been patient with you? What would you say to a friend who thinks that God isn't patient?

32 Accepting Defeat

If I've Told You Once, I've Told You a Thousand Times: You're NOT Going to the Rock Concert, AND THAT'S FINAL!

THE SITUATION

"Hello, is this Mrs. Green? This is Mark and Brian from the KLOS Radio Morning Show."

"Yes, this is Mrs. Green. Can I ask what you're calling about?"

"Mrs. Green, yesterday we received a phone call from your son, Jeremy. He told us that you won't let him go to the upcoming Guns & Roses concert. He called to ask us if we'd give you a call to convince you to let him go."

"Jeremy and I have already discussed this concert many times. I told him that I think he's too young for concerts and that he's not going."

"Oh come on, Mrs. Green! One rock concert isn't going to destroy your son's life. Not every kid is on drugs and alcohol, you know?"

"The answer is no. I've already told Jeremy why I don't want him to go. Besides, the tickets are too expensive. I won't pay for something I don't support."

"Tell you what, Mrs. Green, if you let Jeremy go to the concert, KLOS will give him two Guns & Roses tickets for free! It won't cost you a nickel."

"Yeah, Mom! Free concert tickets! PLEEEAASSEE . . . Can I go?"

"Jeremy, is that you?"

"Yeah, I'm on the other line."

"Jeremy, I don't like this one bit. We've already discussed this. If I've told you once, I've told you a thousand times, you're not going to the concert, and that's final!"

"Mrs. Green, Mrs. Green, what if we throw in a limo and an escort?"

Click.

THE SCRIPTURE

> The father of a righteous man has great joy;
>   he who has a wise son delights in him.
> May your father and mother be glad;
>   may she who gave you birth rejoice!
>   Proverbs 23:24–25

The story you've just read is true. The names have been changed to protect the innocent and to keep me from getting into trouble. Yes, the Mark & Brian Show did call Mrs.

Green, and she wasn't too happy about it. Little did she realize that she was being listened to by thousands of L.A. commuters on their way to work. Knowing when to accept defeat will keep you from chafing your parents raw with incessant pleas and bargains in order to get your way. Knowing when to accept defeat will also keep you from getting grounded. Jeremy was clever; the only problem was that he was clueless about how far he could push his mom. Needless to say, Jeremy got shafted for his creative KLOS stunt. Mrs. Green had drawn her line in the sand, and Jeremy had attempted to cross it. Jeremy did not know how to accept defeat.

There are going to be numerous times when you and your folks don't agree on what kind of clothes are acceptable, who you pick for friends, what curfew time should be, when you can date, and hundreds of other decisions you wish you could make without their input or advice. Sometimes your parents will tell you exactly what their final decision is, with reasons that aren't crystal clear. Then, like The Shaq, they'll head for the rim with a fully-extended, 360 degree slam-dunk *"and that's final!"*

When the discussion ends with a period, you have the choice to accept defeat or to try to throw in your own exclamation point. Exclamation points don't earn extra points. So what do you do? Realize that sometimes you win and sometimes you lose. The Bible says to make your parents glad they gave birth to you. That's why God wants you to be cool to your parents instead of a drag to them. Accepting defeat shows them you're old enough to handle things in a mature way, even when it means backing down from something you really want to do. People who don't know how to accept defeat are setting themselves up for big disasters. Even Mark and Brian had to accept defeat.

THE STRATEGY

When do you have the hardest time accepting defeat from your parents? What was the last situation that caused the most disagreement between you and them? How did the situation resolve itself? What did you learn from it? To better understand what tangles your relationship with your parents, write down the things that you most often disagree about, like you did in chapter five. Then write down your position and the reasons why you feel like you do. Next write down your parents' position and the reasons why they feel like they do. Compare what you just wrote. What possible options do you have that you might not have considered? Is there any way that either side could compromise? What would be the best resolution, a win/win solution, to you and your parents' differences? After you've looked at every possible angle of the situation, and when you aren't in the heat of battle, go talk to your parents about what you wrote and see if you can reach some agreement in these areas.

Rock Music

Turn Down That Music!

THE SITUATION

The Los Angeles Times, Wednesday, February 23, 1994:

A rookie Los Angeles police officer was fatally shot early Tuesday outside a Northridge home by a 17-year-old youth who had killed his father in a dispute over loud music, investigators said. The boy later apparently shot himself to death.

The tragic incident of the senseless deaths of a father, son, and rookie police officer is an extreme example of how rock music can cause tension between you and your parents. Your parents grew up with Jimi Hendrix, the Beatles, Bob Dylan, the Bee Gees, and Barry Manilow. You've grown up with Blind Melon, Madonna, Pearl Jam, MTV, VH–1, U2, Guns & Roses, and a stack of CD/video artists ranging from rap, hip-hop, speed metal, country, alternative, and good ol' rock and roll. Regardless of who's right or wrong, which music is better or worse, rock and roll is here to stay. If you and your parents are going to live together in relative peace, acknowledging your different musical tastes is the first step to facing the music.

But if you're just dying to test out those new, ten-foot tall, dual Marshall amps, a sure-fire way to incur the seething wrath of your dad—who just so happens to be relaxing downstairs by the fire, shoes off, laid back, reading the paper, listening to "Pavarotti Sings Opera's Greatest Hits"—just crank up your stereo to ten on the volume control. "Volume control" is rock and roll's best oxymoron.

THE SCRIPTURE

> Do not be deceived: God cannot be mocked. A man reaps what he sows. The one who sows to please his sinful nature, from that nature will reap destruction; the one who sows to please the Spirit, from the Spirit will reap eternal life.
>
> Galatians 6:7–8

While your parents may scream at you to turn down the music on your stereo or Walkman, there's a more important message that God wants you to tune in to: *You will reap what you sow.* The decisions you make today will affect the rest of your life. The seeds you plant in your life today will grow something positive or negative tomorrow. The important question for you to consider is: What do you want to grow in your life?

Whether it's rock music, watching TV, going to R-rated movies, or reading racy material with lots of photos showing little clothing—whatever you put into your life is the same stuff that will come out of your life. It's called the principle of Garbage In, Garbage Out. Put garbage into your life and garbage will come out. The opposite is also true: Put good things into your life and good things will come out. Depending on what kind of music you listen to, you could be planting good seeds or bad seeds. Back in the Old Testament, the people of Israel were guilty of worshiping a different kind of rock idol in the same way thousands of young people worship rock idols today. The same is true for parents: Teenagers worship and praise rock idols just like parents worship and praise Pavarotti. Parents and young people alike are in danger of replacing a loving, life-giving God with amazing, gifted, modern musicians. Some things never change.

God explicitly says that he wants every person to worship nothing or no one other than him. Tune in to God first. You may have to turn down the volume to hear his voice. And that means turning down the Pavarotti, too!

THE STRATEGY

What kind of seeds are you planting in your life? In every area of your life, you have the chance to sow seeds that produce good fruit or bad fruit. Read over these Scriptures and write down specific ways you can make decisions to plant good seeds and follow Christ. Read John 15 to discover how important your relationship to God is, and how the fruit you bear affects it!

Day-to-Day Decisions

Therefore, I urge you, brothers, in view of God's mercy, to offer your bodies as living sacrifices, holy and pleasing to God— this is your spiritual act of worship. Do not conform any longer to the pattern of this world, but be transformed by the renewing of your mind. Then you will be able to test and approve what God's will is—his good, pleasing and perfect will.

Romans 12:1–2

Friendship Decisions

Wounds from a friend can be trusted,
but an enemy multiplies kisses.
Proverbs 27:6

Future Decisions

Many are the plans in a man's heart,
    but it is the LORD's purpose that prevails.
                                    Proverbs 19:21

Family Decisions

A wise son brings joy to his father,
    but a foolish man despises his mother.
                                    Proverbs 15:20

34 Schemes

What Do You Think I Am ... Stupid?

THE SITUATION

I grew up as a suburban teenage terrorist. My primary clandestine operations involved tactical warfare against my sisters. Outnumbered by five sisters and a younger brother, my only recourse for survival was launching surprise offensive maneuvers. Being a teenage terrorist isn't easy, but it sure is fun.

As a teenage terrorist I always enjoyed the element of surprise, but the types of surprises I gave my sisters were the types they never wanted. Like the time I placed alarm clocks under the bed, desk, and dresser of my sister, Loretta. I set the first clock for 1:00 A.M., the second for 3:00 A.M., and the third for 5:00 A.M.! Or the time my oldest sister, Colleen, received a present in her bed one night. My science experiment, a fetal pig from Mr. Dunn's anatomy/physiology class, was freezing cold in our refrigerator, so I decided to let it sleep in Colleen's bed. My younger brother, Neil, was the frequent recipient of buckets of ice water while he was taking a shower. Every sister at one time or another endured short-sheeted beds (from the end of the bed, fold the bottom sheet in half and tuck in), assorted fishheads in beds (we grew up near the beach), and blanket raids (run into your sister's room while she's asleep and throw a blanket over her; proceed to pummel). A missionary of mercy I was not.

My creating chaos at all hours of the night somehow caused my dad to wake up and groggily inspect what in the world was going on. Staggering down the hallway in his robe, as I quickly released my sister from the Chinese death grip, he'd ask what in the world we were doing yelling and screaming at one o'clock in the morning. "Gee, Dad, Loretta and I are just talking about interpersonal relationships. Is something wrong?" Tired and angry at being awakened in the middle of the night, he'd jump back, "What do you think I am, stupid?" I never liked that question; an honest answer was the wrong answer.

THE SCRIPTURE

> So in everything, do to others what you would have them do to you, for this sums up the Law and the Prophets.
>
> Matthew 7:12

I didn't learn to apply this verse to my life until after I resigned from my role as a teenage terrorist. Doing to my sisters as I would like them to do to me was something that never really entered my mind. I was always scheming, constantly thinking of the next creative or most bizarre prank I could play on them.

I know my mom didn't exactly appreciate a whole clothes basket of shoes dropping on her head when she walked through the kitchen door with two bags of groceries in her arms on April Fool's one year. Nor did Loretta and my best friend, Kevin, enjoy the feeling of getting hit in the rear end with a stinging BB.

Regarding my personal schemes and those of my brother and sisters (I'm not the one who tied Colleen to the lamppost in front of our house right before her date arrived to pick her up), my dad always told us, "It's all fun and games until somebody gets hurt." My dad enjoyed our having fun with one another, but he was sensitive to our hurting each other's feelings. Not hurting each other is at the heart of what Jesus is saying when he tells us to do to one another as we would like done to us.

I've noticed that doing unto others usually gets done back to us, and usually ten times worse. When that happens, tempers rise, screaming starts, and cries of "I didn't get you half as bad as you got me. THAT'S NOT FAIR!" are heard.

Pranks are OK within reason . . . as long as nobody gets hurt. It's important to consider who receives the prank. Are they too sensitive? Too serious? Are they lighthearted? Likely to return the prank? The goal is to be creative, not cruel. (Unlike me in my youth!)

Your parents are not as stupid as you sometimes think they are. They know that the schemes and pranks of today are the hurt feelings and ferocious fights of tomorrow. They know when you've gone too far. While you still have time, do for others as you'd like them to do to you. That includes your brothers and sisters too.

THE STRATEGY

I've already given you plenty of crazy prank ideas (be ready for them to be done back to you!), so here's a list of positive schemes you can do to improve your relationship with your brothers and sisters. Don't be surprised if you catch them off guard by being nice to them. It may take some time for them to realize that you're serious!

Scheming Ideas to Surprise Your Siblings

Take them to lunch.
Go to the movies together.
Go on a double date.
Write a nice letter.
Go running, or work out together.
Plan a prank for your parents.
Clean up their room.
Take their turn doing the dishes.
Help them with homework.
Go to one of their games or school performances.
Bring flowers.
Buy their favorite CD.
Phone them at college.
Listen to their problems.
Compliment them on how they look.
Go camping together.
Dress as nerds and go bowling.

35 Getting Permission

Don't Tell Me— Ask Me!

THE SITUATION

This may be difficult, perhaps even painful, but pretend for a minute that you are a parent. This is your teenager telling you what he (or she) is going to do:

> "Mom, I'm going to go rock climbing with Steve. See ya!"
> "Dad, I'm going to a college party tonight."
> "Don's picking me up in five minutes . . . I've got to get ready now!"
> "No, Tom's parents aren't going to be there. What does it matter?"
> "Ryan is coming over to take me for a ride on his new Ninja motorcycle."
> "The roads will be clear. People drive in the mountains all the time."
> "Everyone's going to be there. Besides, I already told all my friends I'm coming."

"His car looks bad, but it runs fine. He just put a new engine in it."

"After the game, we're going to the dance. After the dance, to Jan's house."

"I'm going to the mall."

"Sue and I are meeting two guys downtown."

"I've got to go now. I'm late. I'll tell you when I get home!"

"I'll call when I get there . . . I promise."

"I need an advance on my allowance. I need ten bucks now."

"Bungee jumping is not as dangerous as it looks."

"I can always do the yard work later."

"More people die in their sleep than rollerblading down hills."

"I'll be back from the beach by four."

"Have you seen my pole? . . I'm going fishing with Bob."

"He just turned nineteen . . . so what?"

"What is there to ask? None of my friends ever have to ask for permission."

THE SCRIPTURE

Ask and it will be given to you; seek and you will find; knock and the door will be opened to you. For everyone who asks receives; he who seeks finds; and to him who knocks, the door will be opened.

Which of you, if his son asks for bread, will give him a stone? Or if he asks for a fish, will give him a snake?

Matthew 7:7–10

How many times have you rushed into the house, late and in a hurry to get ready, screaming to any available parent as you tornado through the living room, "I'm going to Lisa's house. Mike is picking me up in five minutes . . . if anyone calls, tell 'em I'm in the shower!"?

The principle is simple: Don't tell; ask. Asking instead of telling makes a major difference in communicating with your parents. Parents respond to asking and not to telling. The difference between the two is about as wide as the gap between the north and south rims of the Grand Canyon.

Telling your parents what you're going to do is almost the equivalent of telling God what you're going to do. No, your parents are not God and God is not your parents, but both would prefer to be asked instead of being told. Asking shows respect. Telling gives info but no room for input. Your parents want to ask questions before giving permission.

Jesus asks his followers, "What kind of dad would give his son a bunch of rocks if he asked for a loaf of bread, or if he asked for a fish, would he give him a snake?" Jesus isn't talking about getting permission to go to the movies, but the principle is clear: Receiving from your parents, whether it's permission or material things, is related to asking, not telling.

When you *tell* your parents what you're going to do, it's like using a megaphone instead of a telephone. Your parents get blasted and the only person heard is you. The next time you're tempted to tell your parents where you're going or what you're doing, just ask instead.

THE STRATEGY

This time let's put your parents to work. Have your mom or dad read this chapter. *Ask* them to put their brains to work by thinking of the situations when you have told them what you're planning on doing. Have them write down three reasons why they would prefer you ask for permission. What are the things you like to do that they are most hesitant to let you do? What are better ways to communicate with one another? Talk about how this conversation can be helpful for getting permission to do things in the future.

36   *Example*

Leave Your Little Brother Alone. . . . He's Smaller than You!

THE SITUATION

Neil used to get me in so much trouble. Sure, there were plenty of times when I pummeled him, digging his face into the ground to make facial impressions in bas-relief. And there was that one time when I accidentally landed a big wad of spit right on his face.

Neil and I were having a friendly wrestling match, and as usual, I was on top of him, pinning him to the ground as if I were a Roman gladiator. Sitting on his stomach with my knees holding down his arms, I proceeded to give him a smattering of "sternum thumps." After pounding his chest, I cleared my throat, producing a large amount of saliva mixed with stringy chunks of throat dough.

"You'd better not do your spit trick on me," he screamed. Hee-hee-hee!

In vain, Neil tried to break the hold of steel I had on him. Leaning over his face, I slowly drooled my bungee "loogie" over him. Sucking it back up a couple of times, I proceeded to let the stringy loogie get longer and longer. And longer.

"I'm going to kill you if that thing drops on me! Stop it!" Neil protested.

"Settle down, it's not going to break. I'm a pro at this." So I thought.

The wet, gooey loogie snapped and landed on Neil's face. He was not happy. I had to keep him pinned for a long time before he cooled down.

For all the awful schemes I inflicted on Neil, what always got me into trouble was his one-liner, "Mom, Dad, Joey's hitting me." I'd be standing three feet from Neil, and he'd slap his leg and scream, "OW! Joey's hitting me." My mom would run in from the other room and say in a loud voice, "How many times have I told you not to hit your younger brother . . . he's smaller than you!"

"He's lying . . . I didn't touch him!" I'd scream in protest.

"Don't you raise your voice to me," my mom warned me.

Neil stood there with a devilish grin on his face, watching me get in trouble. Hee-hee-hee!

THE SCRIPTURE

Don't let anyone look down on you because you are young, but set an example for the believers in speech, in life, in love, in faith and in purity.

1 Timothy 4:12

My parents had a vested interest in keeping Neil alive, but the main reason why they told me not to beat, hit, slap, and thump him was simply so I could be a good example to him. I figured that if my four older sisters pounded on me, then I was allowed to pound on Neil. Four on one wasn't fair, so what was wrong with one on one? My parents didn't go for either one.

Not only is picking on someone smaller than you not a fair fight, but it also destroys the possibility of having a brother or sister as a friend. *Why in the world would I want my bratty little sister as a friend?* Why not?

When I was growing up, I don't know why, but most of the time I viewed my brothers and sisters as adversaries. Only when I needed something from them were they considered allies. As I look back on it now, I really didn't benefit much from getting my hair pulled out by the roots, my arms scratched to the bone, and my shins kicked purple. Fighting didn't get me anything or anywhere. Did my parents know something I didn't?

As a follower of Jesus Christ, you have the opportunity to set an example your brothers and sisters can follow. When you think about pounding your brother through the earth's core, ask yourself if that's an example you would want him to show others. *But you don't know my brother!* No, I don't, but a simple truth remains: Your brothers and sisters will want to be like you, or they will want to be anything *but* like you. Which would you prefer? Having your brothers and sisters follow your example is the best compliment you could ever receive.

THE STRATEGY

If you still plan on fighting with your brother or sister, at least you could start the fight by giving them the advantage. Here are some creative ways to have a fair fight.

Bigger person has one hand tied behind back.
Bigger person has to fight on knees.
Bigger person has to use a blindfold.

If you fight in a pool, smaller person gets to use arm floaties.

Smaller person stands on chair.

Smaller person gets feather pillow. Bigger person gets polyester.

Smaller person gets a ten-second headstart.

Smaller person gets longer sword.

Smaller person gets hose. Bigger person gets bucket of water.

Smaller person gets first choice of weapon.

Bigger person has to crawl.

Smaller person gets to say "Uncle" six times. Bigger person gets to say it three times.

When I Was a Kid, I Used to Walk Ten Miles to School in Three Feet of Snow Holding a Warm Potato in My Freezing Cold Hands, and I Ate the Potato for Lunch!

THE SITUATION

Our poor parents. It seems like every kid has a mom and dad who grew up in the Great Depression and walked to school in the snow holding a warm potato in their freezing cold hands, and later ate the potato for lunch. If you believe that one, then I want to sell you some choice property on the moon, swampland in Florida, a bottle of Never-Wash-Your-Car-Again-Carwax, two Flobee haircutters, one Thighmaster, a set of Ginzu knives complete with apple peeler, a NordicTrak to go nowhere fast, and a SoloFlex machine to give you a body to die for. Tell you what, buy all this now and I'll even throw in the Ronco blender for free!

How have your parents blown things out of proportion lately? Have they said crazy things like . . .

"You're NEVER home on time."

"You ALWAYS run off before helping with the dishes."

"When I was a kid, I had a part-time job EVERY summer."

"You do NOTHING around here."

"Can't you do ANYTHING right?"

"When are you going to LEARN your lesson?"

"Surely you can think of SOMETHING to do with your free time?"

"Don't even THINK of leaving this house tonight!"

Geez, where do they learn all this stuff? How come teenagers get a bad rap for exaggerating? How come parents never get in trouble for saying things like that?

THE SCRIPTURE

Dear children, let us not love with words or tongue but with actions and in truth.

1 John 3:18

OK, we all know that parents tend to exaggerate. When they're upset, parents tend to use words that you're not allowed to use, extreme words like *always, never, nothing, anything, every.* Because parents are human, just like you and I, they tend to exaggerate.

There could be all sorts of reasons why parents exaggerate instead of using the calm, measured, carefully selected words you *always* use. Maybe your dad had a bad day at work, and he was upset that you didn't mow the lawn like you said you would. So, your dad used the *never* word. Maybe your mom got sick of your leaving your cereal bowl in the sink, so she whipped out the *always* word. Because your parents have feelings, they can *sometimes* get upset over things that seem minor to you. So what do you do?

The apostle John gives some good advice when he tells us not to love with lots of words but with actions. I think parents sometimes feel unloved. They sometimes feel like you don't give a rip about how they feel. When you make a commitment to do something but don't follow through, then parents resort to extremes to get your attention. That's not always the best way to handle situations, but hey, not even your parents are perfect.

You can show your parents that you really love them by your actions. Saying "I love you" is easy; acting like it is a whole lot harder. When you're willing to stick to your commitments, that shows your folks that you love them. Sure you're going to mess up once in a while, but the long-term goal is to love faithfully and consistently, not perfectly. When you tell your folks you love them with your actions, then they'll know *you're* not exaggerating when you tell them with your words.

THE STRATEGY

Get together with your folks and talk about the words you all can use when a conflict comes up. Mutually agree not to use the *always, never, nothing,* or *anything* words in your discussions. Also, pick out any other negative words that your parents and you tend to use during disputes. Agree that anyone who uses extreme or negative language during a fight has to take the other person to the movies when it's all over. That's a bet you'll want to win!

38 Last Resorts

Over My Dead Body!

THE SITUATION

Almost every year in school, the teacher would ask each person in my class to stand up and tell the rest of the class what kind of work our fathers did. I loved the reaction I got out of my classmates when it was my turn to proudly divulge my father's occupation: *My dad is a funeral director. He buries people for a living.* A dead calm would silence the entire class. Patiently, I would wait for the incredulous statements and morbid questions that would always follow:

"Your dad does what?"

"Eeewww . . . that's gross!"

"NO WAY!"

"Do they really drain the blood out of the body?"

"Does he ever bring his work home?"

"Do they really hang 'em on meat hooks like they do in the movies?"

"Does your dad bury animals too? I once had a pet that died and we . . ."

"I want my mommy!"

"Isn't your dad sad all the time?"

"Have you ever seen a dead body?"

"I'm going to get cremated. I'm not going to have worms crawling all over me!"

"I think I'm going to throw up."

Yes, my dad is a mortician. I am a mortician's son and proud of it. How many kids do you know who got to come to school in a limousine? How many kids do you know who occasionally got to come to school in a hearse? When my dad let us stuff forty-eight junior high friends into the limo to take us to school, I was the most popular kid on the block!

THE SCRIPTURE

> During the days of Jesus' life on earth, he offered up prayers and petitions with loud cries and tears to the one who could save him from death, and he was heard because of his reverent submission. Although he was a son, he learned obedience from what he suffered.
>
> Hebrews 5:7–8

When I gave my dad some outrageous request, and his response was "Not over my dead body," I knew he meant business. He was able to say that with more authority than anyone I've ever known. My dad's ultimatum was the type of ultimatum you paid attention to.

Why do parents give ultimatums and last resorts? Why do parents say things like, "If you go out that door, you're never coming back," and "If you want to keep breathing, you'd better shut your mouth!" (I still haven't figured that one out!) Parents dish out ultimatums when they think teenagers have stopped listening to sound reasoning. They resort to unsound reasoning. I know it sounds crazy, but that's the way moms and dads tend to operate.

Jesus had to learn how to be obedient to his parents, just as you do. He was able to keep a good relationship with his earthly parents and, at the same time, learn how to follow his heavenly Father's will for his life. That's the same challenge you have as a Christian. You can save yourself a truckload of ultimatums by learning how to be obedient to your folks. It may involve some misunderstandings, tears, hassles, and conflicts, but like Jesus, you can come away with a better relationship with God and your parents. That's an ultimatum you don't need to be afraid of!

THE STRATEGY

Obeying your parents isn't always easy. Most of the time, it's plain hard work. But it does have all sorts of powerful benefits. Study the following verses that relate to the benefits of being obedient to God and your parents. Write down specific ways you can improve your relationship with God and your parents by applying the verses to your life.

And this is love: that we walk in obedience to his commands. As you have heard from the beginning, his command is that you walk in love.

2 John 6

Be careful to obey all these regulations I am giving you, so that it may always go well with you and your children after you, because you will be doing what is good and right in the eyes of the LORD your God.

Deuteronomy 12:28

It is the LORD your God you must follow, and him you must revere. Keep his commands and obey him; serve him and hold fast to him.

Deuteronomy 13:4

But be very careful to keep the commandment and the law that Moses the servant of the LORD gave you: to love the LORD your God, to walk in all his ways, to obey his commands, to hold fast to him and to serve him with all your heart and all your soul.

Joshua 22:5

Give me understanding, and I will keep your law
and obey it with all my heart.

Psalm 119:34

Your statutes are wonderful;
therefore I obey them.
Psalm 119:129

If you obey my commands, you will remain in my love, just as I have obeyed my Father's commands and remain in his love.

John 15:10

If you love me, you will obey what I command.

John 14:15

Jesus replied, "If anyone loves me, he will obey my teaching. My Father will love him, and we will come to him and make our home with him."

John 14:23

39 | Listening to God

Do You Have a Hearing Problem?

THE SITUATION

"Where am I? What happened?" I asked as my friend's face swirled around in front of me like a kaleidoscope.

"Joey, look at me. Look at me—yeah, right here. You just hit your face on the diving board! Are you OK?"

As the saying goes, I really didn't know what hit me. It was Saturday afternoon, and my friends and I were playing football in the pool. We had spent the day hanging out together and now were cooling off. We played the usual pool games like Marco Polo, chicken fights, and wrestling, and performed diving board antics, when I pulled the wildest stunt of all. It was supposed to have been a simple back flip. I had previously done thousands of back flips. This one was no different except that when I jumped, I jumped up instead of out. A few more feet and I could have completed a whole 360 and landed on my feet again. Instead, the rebounding white diving board met me with a hard, wet slap in the face.

All I heard from my friends was laughter and disbelief over what an incredible *ABC Wild World of Sports* "agony of defeat" maneuver I had just executed. My friends were laughing and I was drowning. A couple guys swam over and pulled me out. I had no clue as to what was going on. The only thing I was conscious of was my aching, throbbing face, which felt like it had been hit by a baseball. I thought someone had thrown the football in my face. I wished someone had merely thrown a football at my face.

Out of the pool, my friends tried to get my attention, but all I could hear were whistling cuckoo birds and gonging bells. I kept saying, "What happened? What happened?" Everyone tried to explain what had happened, but I was mentally incapacitated. Finally, I stared my friends in the face and said, "Where am I? How'd I get here?" All my friends looked at each other and agreed, "He's out of it. He doesn't hear a word we're saying. We'd better get him to the hospital."

THE SCRIPTURE

Then I heard the voice of the Lord saying, "Whom shall I send? And who will go for us?"

And I said, "Here am I. Send me!"

Isaiah 6:8

The day I hit my face on the diving board, I couldn't hear a word my friends were saying. Not only was my face killing me, I also had a concussion that made my brain feel like Jell-O brand gelatin. Having a concussion is a pretty good reason for not listening to what others are saying.

If you're reading this chapter right now, there's a good chance you don't have a concussion. Your parents may accuse you of not being a very good listener, and I can understand why. Listening to your folks means you can't go out on a school night or you may have to clean your bedroom. Listening involves obeying what your parents tell you to do. That's not always fun.

Listening to God may not always seem to be fun either. Sometimes God tells you not to do certain things that you want to do, because he knows those things can mess you up. There are also lots of things God tells you to do: Wait for sex until marriage; treat your body with respect by not putting drugs or alcohol into it; choose friends who are a good influence; listen to your parents. Following God means listening to God, and listening often isn't easy.

Isaiah was a guy who heard God's voice. Isaiah listened to God. God was looking for someone to send on a mission, and because Isaiah listened, he was able to volunteer for the position. When you listen to God, you put yourself in the position of discovering the wonderful character of who God is. If you have to decide whether to get hit in the face with a diving board or listen to God, take the second choice. It doesn't hurt as much.

THE STRATEGY

Reading through the Book of Psalms in the Old Testament is a good way to discover how to listen to God. The writers are people just like you who have big questions, nagging doubts, and all sorts of confusing feelings that they pour out to God. Psalms will help you listen to God. This book is filled with praises, prayers, confessions of sin, thanksgiving, and rejoicing over who God is. Take some time right now and read a couple psalms to discover what God is saying to you. Listening to God will change your life as you learn to love him more and follow him in all you do.

40 Excellence

I Know You Can Do Better than That!

THE SITUATION

Report cards reflect whether or not studying is important in your life. If the grades on your report card aren't as high as your parents think they should be, then they'll probably sit you down for the old priority talk. Your report card won't show how much time you spent talking instead of studying at Steve's house, and it won't register the number of Sega high scores you achieved before cracking your books. But your report card will reflect the cumulative grade for the tests taken, papers written, speeches given, and homework completed. Grades can be protested, but most of the time, grades are set in stone. Your dad will spend 15.8 seconds studying the little capital letters on your report card: B-, C, C, B, D, C-, A. The A in gym class won't count. And he'll say, "I know you can do better than that."

Missing a few practices can also mean the difference between winning and losing a game. Skipping practice to go eat pizza with friends or visit your girlfriend will get you benched by your coach. Or maybe you're in the game, but your mind is somewhere else. Losing your concentration because you're thinking of all the people watching you in the stands is almost as bad as being physically absent. Whether you're physically or mentally absent in competition, neither will win matches. After watching you flounder in the field or gym, your dad may hand you the hard-to-hear-advice: I know you can do better than that.

Your attitude around the house may be just one more thing that needs improvement. You bark at your brother like a dog, you slam your sister into the wall for looking at you, and you snap at your mom for asking how your day went. You know you're going to hear about it later; what'll your folks say?

"I know you can do better than that."

THE SCRIPTURE

Finally, brothers, whatever is true, whatever is noble, whatever is right, whatever is pure, whatever is lovely, whatever is admirable—if anything is excellent or praiseworthy—think about such things. Whatever you have learned or received or heard from me, or seen in me—put it into practice. And the God of peace will be with you.

Philippians 4:8–9

Though it may sound like criticism, nagging, or a cut-down when your parents tell you that they know you can do better, they tell you because it's true. When you don't strive to do your best, your parents will tell you that you're settling for being average, mediocre, so-so, lukewarm, and 50-50. They know flat Coke when they see it. Your folks know you can do better than that, and so do you.

Why do you settle for second best? What is the part inside of you that wants the easy way out? How can you be so motivated in some areas of your life, but so apathetic in others? Your parents see your potential and your talents. Believe it or not, they see special abilities in you that you may not even recognize in yourself. That's why when you settle for being physically, mentally, or spiritually lazy, your parents step in to light a fire underneath your wet wood. Sure, there are times when you get burnt out and tired, but lighting your fire is one of your parents' primary roles. If they don't keep pushing you to do your best now, then someday when they're not around anymore, you might not be motivated to pick up a match and light your own fire.

Living a life of excellence doesn't mean getting straight As or being on every winning team. Living a life of excellence is doing your best with what God has given you, and once you've done your best, to give the credit to God. Striving for excellence first begins with thinking right thoughts. That's why the apostle Paul says to fill your mind with whatever is true, noble, right, pure, lovely, or admirable. If you can think of anything that is excellent or worth praising, then that's the stuff you want to think about. Once you're working on thinking right thoughts, the next step is to practice what you're thinking about. That's what pursuing excellence is all about. Once you choose to live a life of excellence, then you'll know you're giving God your best, and you'll have his peace to prove it.

THE STRATEGY

Paul's challenge to live a life of excellence can help you do better where you might have slacked off. Write down one or two specific areas of your life that you want to work on. After the following attributes listed by Paul, write specific ways that you can change your attitudes or actions. You know you can do better, and Jesus Christ is the one who will help you. He is patient, understanding, and kind. He understands you even when your parents don't.

Example: I need to watch my tongue. I've said a lot of bad things lately.

Whatever is true: I won't lie to my parents.

Whatever is noble: I'm not going to gossip about Jennifer.

Whatever is right:

Whatever is pure:

Whatever is lovely:

Whatever is admirable:

Whatever is excellent:

Whatever is praiseworthy:

This week, I'm going to practice:

41 Breaking Up

I Know How You Feel

THE SITUATION

You've been lying on your bed for over an hour, crying, reading the same, tear-stained letter over and over. Tears won't stop flowing. You never realized you could love someone so much. The special feelings you've felt the past few weeks have rocketed you to wonderful peaks of excitement and joy. You thought these feelings would never go away—until now.

A lonely, gnawing feeling rips at your heart. Your throat is raw from crying so much, and your watery eyes are bloodshot and puffy. You're a mess. Your stomach is killing you, and you feel like you're going to throw up.

You wonder as you say to yourself, "I can't believe it's just *over!* I thought things were going great between us! What happened? Just last week, he told me that he loved me. Was he lying? Is it over . . . just like that?"

You hear quiet footsteps, and your bedroom door opens a crack. Quickly, you stuff your face into the pile of pillows on your bed. You don't want anyone to know what has happened.

"Knock, knock, honey, are you in here? Hey, hey, what's wrong?"

Your mom slowly sits down on your bed. She sees the tear-blotched letter crumpled in your hand. Gently, she begins to stroke your hair as she waits for you to pull your head out of the pillows. After a minute or so, your eyes meet, but not a word needs to be said. Throwing yourself into your mom's warm lap, all the poisonous hurt and confusing feelings come pouring out of you like the raging, pounding surf of a cold winter storm. As you cry in uncontrollable sobs, your mom simply pats your back and reassures you with her tender words.

THE SCRIPTURE

> As a mother comforts her child,
> so will I comfort you.
> Isaiah 66:13

There's nothing better than a good cry. When you're hurting, confused, and angry about why the person you care so much about just dumped you, the best thing you can do is cry.

I remember when my first girlfriend, Christy, dumped me in the eighth grade. At first, she liked me, but I didn't like her. After a couple weeks, we started dating, and I discovered that I really liked her. We had been going steady for a month, and the Niguel Hills Junior High Valentines Dance was quickly approaching. To show Christy how much I liked her, I bought her one of my sister's necklaces for twenty-eight bucks. (That was a deal!)

The dance came, and I gave Christy my heart with the necklace. I was so excited I felt like leapfrogging over Mt. Everest. What went wrong next, I still don't have a clue about.

After the dance, all our friends went out for pizza, and before I knew it, Christy broke up with me. Feeling rejected and like a complete idiot, I stood outside the pizza place and cried like a pathetic loser.

It doesn't matter if you're a guy or girl. When someone breaks up with you, the pain of a broken heart isn't gender specific. Though it may not be cool to cry if you're a guy, putting on a big mask by pretending to be bullet-proof resilient isn't too cool either. Girls and guys alike need to know that it's OK to cry when their feelings are hurt. Crying is God's way of flushing out pain.

Believe it or not, your mom or dad may know how you feel. Chances are that they have had a few breakups of their own. Even though they might not know *exactly* how you're feeling, they can still help you get through your hurt. Moms and dads can make a big difference when you're feeling the pain of rejection. Just like your folks can comfort you, so can your Father in heaven. God knows what the pain of rejection is like. Jesus knows how it feels to be rejected by the ones closest to him. Jesus knows how you feel.

THE STRATEGY

Do you know someone who is hurting from a recent breakup with a boyfriend or girlfriend? Is it you? A friend? God can comfort you or them as a mother comforts her child. Read the following verses about God's compassion and comfort. How can these verses make a difference in your life in light of losing a recent love? What do these verses say about God's unconditional love for you? Whom can you share this chapter with as a way to help and cheer them?

> As a father has compassion on his children,
>   so the LORD has compassion on those who fear him.
> Psalm 103:13

The LORD is gracious and righteous;
our God is full of compassion.

Psalm 116:5

The LORD is good to all;
he has compassion on all he has made.

Psalm 145:9

Praise be to the God and Father of our Lord Jesus Christ, the Father of compassion and the God of all comfort, who comforts us in all our troubles, so that we can comfort those in any trouble with the comfort we ourselves have received from God.

2 Corinthians 1:3

But you, O LORD, are a compassionate and gracious God, slow to anger, abounding in love and faithfulness.

Psalm 86:15

Waiting

We'll See

THE SITUATION

Your friend at school has just invited you to go skiing this weekend. This is your chance to get away for the weekend with a group of cool guys, and you can't wait to ask for your parents' permission. They've let you do lots of things like this in the past, so you figure this one will be a cinch. No problem.

"It's already Thursday and your friend is just asking you to go now?" your dad asks with a funny look on his face.

"Well, yeah. What's the big deal? He just found out that his parents would let him have the cabin."

"You mean his parents won't be there?" your dad asks with that funny look now turning serious.

"Uh, no . . . like I said, John invited four of us to go skiing to his folks' cabin."

"But you didn't say that his parents wouldn't be there."

"No, but you didn't ask," you nervously respond to your dad's increasingly pointed questions.

"Since when have your mother and I allowed you to go to the mountains by yourself with four other guys?"

"I know this is the first time, but you've let me go on lots of trips before."

"Those were either youth group trips or trips that had parents."

"I know, but it's about time you trusted me alone with my friends. I'm sixteen now; I'm not a baby anymore."

"No one's calling you a baby. It's just that I don't like your traveling on mountain roads in the snow and ice all by yourself."

"Dad! I'm not going alone . . . I'm going with four other guys. John's done a lot of driving in the mountains, and he knows what he's doing. Why can't I go?"

Your dad is wrestling with this one. He knows that you'll be fine, but there are a number of things for him to consider. After a short pause, he says, "First let me talk to your mother and see what she thinks. I'm not saying yes, and I'm not saying, no. We'll see."

THE SCRIPTURE

> I wait for the LORD, my soul waits,
> and in his word I put my hope.
> Psalm 130:5

"We'll see" puts you in the most torturous, precarious, nail-biting position a parent could ever put you in. When my mom or dad used to inflict those words on me, I'd impatiently respond, "What is there to see? Why can't we make a decision right now? I've given you all the facts. What more do you need to know?"

If there was anything that bothered me more than hearing the words, "No, you can't go," it was hearing the words, "We'll see." "We'll see" leaves you in the embarrassing spot of having to call your friend back and say, "I don't know if I can go yet. My parents are talking about it, but I won't know until they know, and we both know that could take forever."

Waiting for your parents to make a decision to let you go out with your friends is a test of your patience and character. The same is true for your relationship with God. You pray and ask God all sorts of requests, but you have to wait for him to get back to you. The difference is you know you can go into the living room to pester your parents, but you can't storm into heaven and demand an answer from God.

Waiting for God involves trusting that he has your best interests in mind. Waiting for God isn't easy to do, and some times the answer he gives you is just like your folks' "We'll see." God has perfect timing, and being in his will means going by his clock, not yours. As you wait for God, he develops your patience and creates in you a character like Jesus Christ's. Becoming like Jesus is worth waiting for.

THE STRATEGY

What makes it so difficult to be patient? How do your parents make you wait for a decision? When was the worst time you had to wait for a decision from them? How do you respond when your parents tell you that you can't do something you want to do? How is waiting for God similar to waiting for your parents? How is it different? Write down positive ways to respond to your mom or dad when they say, "We'll see."

Example: When waiting to see if I can go to my friend's play tonight, I won't

throw a tantrum
throw my little brother
throw around the wrong types of words

But, I will

pray for patience
agree to wait
work at having a good attitude
listen to my parents' answer before reacting to it

43 Fear

Just Wait 'Til Your Father Gets Home!

THE SITUATION

Kathy and I both received BigWheels for Christmas. She trashed hers within a few weeks; I took care of mine. Then Kathy wanted my BigWheel.

When we were kids, the big rage was BigWheels. A Big-Wheel was a round, yellow cart that had two BIG red wheels with a seat in between. To operate a BigWheel, all you had to do was sit down and spin the handles connected to the wheels. You could do all sorts of spins, go forward, go backward, and bash anything from any direction. BigWheels were like manually operated bumper cars. BigWheels were cool. That's why I took care of mine.

One day, I was innocently cruising my BigWheel down the cement path that divided the lawn in our backyard when Kathy walked up and said, "Let me use your BigWheel. Mine's broken."

I said, "No," and proceeded down the path.

"Give me your BigWheel," Kathy said in a louder voice. "No way, it's mine!" I shouted back. "You busted yours . . . you're not going to bust mine too!"

Kathy walked over to the log pile. I walked over to the log pile too. Kathy picked up a log. I picked up one too.

"Now let me use your BigWheel or I'm going to hit you with this log!"

"It's my BigWheel, not yours! I don't have to let you use it if I don't want to!"

Kathy moved toward me, log in hand. I stepped back, log in hand. She advanced. I tripped over a sprinkler head and fell down next to my BigWheel. My body fell on the grass, but my hand was lying on the cement path. Kathy dropped the log. On the cement path. On my hand. Right on my pinkie. As my mom rushed me to the hospital, can you guess what she said to Kathy?

THE SCRIPTURE

For you did not receive a spirit that makes you a slave again to fear, but you received the Spirit of sonship. And by him we cry, "Abba, Father."

Romans 8:15

When was the last time you really got in trouble for something you didn't mean to do? There are all kinds of things that you mean to do, but in the middle of doing something you mean to do, something usually happens that you didn't mean to do—you know what I mean? Like when your sister destroys a tape of yours that she took without asking, what do you do? You slug her. That's something you mean to do. The only problem is that when you slug her and she swings back, she misses and slams her knuckles into the wall. Now she is crying hysterically, and you get in trouble for her hurting herself. You didn't mean for her to hit the wall; you only meant to hit her.

Almost every teenager I know has lived in the fear of waiting for Dad to get home. Maybe your dad isn't around, so instead you live in fear of waiting for Mom to get home. Either way, fear is fear, and you know that whenever the object of your fear gets home, you're history. The one thing worse than fear itself is the waiting. What can be worse than waiting for your father to get home when you're in trouble?

God and your parents are different. When you fear your parents for something you did wrong, it's because you know you're going to get in trouble. You may fear that God operates the same way, but he doesn't. If you have a relationship with Jesus Christ, then there's nothing to fear about your heavenly Father. Through faith, when you believe in Christ you are welcomed into the family of God. You become a son or daughter of the King. Paul says you do not receive a spirit of fear but can now run to God like a little boy or girl runs to his or her daddy. If you're going to run, run into the arms of God. There's nothing to fear with him holding you tight.

THE STRATEGY

What is the worst thing you ever got in trouble for? Knowing that you have a heavenly Father who loves you and forgives you when you make mistakes can change your life in ways you never imagined. Using a pencil, write down the blunders that you've done lately. Read over the following verses about forgiveness. After confessing your sins to God and receiving his forgiveness, erase what you just wrote. In God's eyes you are completely forgiven. He sees your sins no more.

In him we have redemption through his blood, the forgiveness of sins, in accordance with the riches of God's grace.

Ephesians 1:7

For he has rescued us from the dominion of darkness and brought us into the kingdom of the Son he loves, in whom we have redemption, the forgiveness of sins.

Colossians 1:13–14

Bear with each other and forgive whatever grievances you may have against one another. Forgive as the Lord forgave you.

Colossians 3:13

For I will forgive their wickedness
and will remember their sins no more.

Hebrews 8:12

If we confess our sins, he is faithful and just and will forgive us our sins and purify us from all unrighteousness.

1 John 1:9

44   *Peer Pressure*

Would You Jump off a Bridge If Everyone Else Was Doing It?

THE SITUATION

As I mentioned before, I grew up at the beach. All summer long, my friends and I hung out at the beach, surfing, playing volleyball, annoying girls, and jumping off cliffs–very high cliffs.

After the morning surf was blown out, we'd get bored lying in the sand until someone would shout, "Hey, let's go cliff-jumping." Cheers would rise up from the gang as everyone grabbed their shoes. To get to the cliffs, we had to walk north along the beach and then walk a stretch of rocks for half a mile. Once we reached the Monarch Bay point, a big rocky out-cropping with huge waves that smashed against a natural sea-wall, we jumped into the water to reach the other side of rocks. Reaching the other side wasn't a walk on soft white sand.

To avoid getting smashed like fish bait against the rocks, we had to wait for a lull in between the sets of waves, jump into the water and swim about a hundred meters to the other side. Time it just right and you were fine. Time it just wrong and you got slammed against the seawall. All this and you weren't even at the cliffs yet!

On each cliff-jumping adventure, there was always at least one of us who got slammed against the razor-sharp barnacles of the rocks. If you were cut on the rocks, you earned both laughter and respect for getting caught between sets and living to tell about it. Once on the other side, it was a quick scramble up the rocks to the Three Arch Bay cliffs. The cliffs are notorious among locals as the source of an awesome adrenaline rush of jumping madness. The cliff jump spots range from ten feet to seventy-five feet. My friends and I usually picked the fifty-foot jump spot because its launch pad was the furthest out from the cliff wall.

Standing on the launch pad, looking down at the deep green-blue water below, my pre-flight mental checklist went something like this: *Relax, stay calm, jump out away from the rock, wave arms for balance, don't lean over like Tom Smith just did, legs together, feet pointed down, arms held at side at impact . . . one, two, three . . . JUMP!*

THE SCRIPTURE

> Wisdom will save you from the ways of wicked men,
>> from men whose words are perverse,
> who leave the straight paths
>> to walk in dark ways,
> who delight in doing wrong
>> and rejoice in the perverseness of evil,
> whose paths are crooked
>> and who are devious in their ways.
>
> Proverbs 2:12 –15

I never jumped off a bridge, like my dad warned me about, but I jumped off the Three Arch Bay cliffs plenty of times. He never said, "Would you jump off a cliff if everyone else was doing it?" He always used the word "bridge." Maybe if he would have used the word "cliff," I would have listened to him.

Though my friends and I went on numerous cliff-jumping expeditions, I knew what my dad was saying. He was talking about peer pressure. He was talking about not doing stupid things just because everyone else was doing them.

In junior and senior high, I gave in to peer pressure a lot. I also inflicted a lot of peer pressure on others. In seventh grade, I tried cigarettes and alcohol for the first time. In eighth grade, I started smoking pot. Using drugs and alcohol didn't seem as risky as jumping off a bridge. Besides, my friends and I were having a lot of fun—or so I thought.

By the time I was a sophomore in high school, I was partied out. I thought, *Is this all there is to life? . . . drinking . . . partying . . . girls?* After my girlfriend broke up with me, I really began to question the lifestyle I was living. I was supposedly having fun. I was popular. I had lots of friends, but I wasn't happy.

Now I understand what my dad was talking about. I wish I would have listened a little bit earlier. My friends weren't at fault. I was. I chose to make bad decisions and be a bad influence on others. I didn't push anyone off a cliff, but I sure got a few people to the launch pad so they could jump on their own.

THE STRATEGY

Peer pressure can be subtle and deceptive. It begins with a little compromise here and a little compromise there. Before you know it, you can be doing things you thought you'd never do. What kinds of peer pressure do you feel most susceptible to? What is the hardest area of temptation for you to resist? Which of your friends value the same things you value? How can God help you to stand up to people who want to drag you down? Write down some creative ways you can stand up against peer pressure.

Example: John always asks me to help him cheat on tests.

Tell John to go cliff-jumping.
Change my seat in class.
Offer to help John study and learn the material.

Example: My friends pressure me to go drink with them.

Suggest a fun and creative alternative.
Have a serious talk with my friends about what I stand for and why.
Find new friends.

Discipline

Don't Forget to Brush Your Teeth and Floss

THE SITUATION

Whining, high-speed power tools. Disgusting fluoride treatments. Numb lips. Water dribbling down my chin. Sharp metal instruments. Pain. Going to the dentist ranks on my Least Favorite Things to Do list somewhere between walking on broken shards of glass and listening to disco music. Just thinking about that raspy, tongue-grabbing suction tube strikes at the wiggly root of every nerve in my mouth.

Our dentist's waiting room, filled with wrinkled and worn *National Geographic, People, Time,* and *Highlights* magazines, was also covered with photographs of heavy machinery, drills, and pioneer mining operations. That was always disconcerting to a scared little kid. Then there was that little creepy, foggy, sliding window that opened for 1.3 seconds with a voice behind it that barked, "NEXT!" Did anybody ever know if that was a human voice or not? And why, I always wondered, did I see children enter through a door but never exit?

Sitting in a dentist's chair is an exercise in self-control. Not only are dentists' chairs designed to make you squirm, but there also is no other piece of furniture that comes with a piece of paper behind your head; a halogen, airplane-landing light in your face; and seatbelts to strap you in. The only thing that was kind of cool about the dentist's chair was the automatic cup refiller that you always thought would overflow but never did. After being shot up with enough Novocain to put a horse to sleep, getting two or three teeth drilled to the core, and receiving a whiff of burning tooth dust, the only thing I looked forward to hearing was "Rinse." Oh, and there was always that wonderful free gift the dentist gave you for all the pain he just put you through—a toothbrush.

THE SCRIPTURE

No discipline seems pleasant at the time, but painful. Later on, however, it produces a harvest of righteousness and peace for those who have been trained by it.

Hebrews 12:11

Why have your parents been bugging you to brush and floss your teeth all these years? Is it because of the dentist's bill? Yes and no. My mom once told me that if I didn't start taking care of my teeth, then I was going to be responsible to pay for the bill. Have you ever got that line? After three or four trips to the dentist and eight to ten fillings later, I wised up to the fact that I had something to do with *why* the dentist was sticking a twenty-gauge drill bit in my mouth.

If you're wondering about the relationship between dentists and discipline, here's a question you might want to consider: Do you want to live with the pain of discipline or the pain of regret? Does that strike a nerve? Besides avoiding having to fork over big bucks for dentists' bills, my parents were trying to teach me a lesson about taking care of myself. The consequences of not brushing and flossing are drilling and capping.

We make the choice to live with the pain of discipline or the pain of regret in our relationship with God, too. How many times have you said something you wish you wouldn't have said, but because you didn't discipline your tongue, someone else got hurt? What about studying for tests? "Lord, if you just see me through this math final, I promise I'll study all summer long!" Or what about promises you make that you really never intend to keep? The Bible says it's better to live with the pain of discipline than the pain of regret. Why? Because regret produces nothing but anxiety and heartache. Discipline produces right living (righteousness) and peace for those who have been trained by it. Regret reminds you of what you're not. Discipline makes you who God wants you to be. Regret is a lousy motivator, but discipline creates the kind of strong character God wants to develop in you. I know flossing—discipline—is a difficult art form, but it's better to live with bleeding gums than a bleeding heart.

THE STRATEGY

1. Make a list of the areas in your life you are least disciplined in.
2. Write down a well-defined purpose for wanting to grow in this area. You need a clear purpose as to why you want to change in order to make a significant, lasting change.
3. Write down all the things that easily distract you from doing what's most important.
4. Write down all the benefits that could result from being more disciplined in these areas.
5. Set a simple, attainable goal for each one of these areas. Each goal needs to be specific regarding time and place.

6. Ask someone to help you with reaching your goals, someone who can support you and ask you how you're doing.

Example:

Area I'm going to work on: Homework.
Purpose: To do better in school. Raise my GPA. Become a brain surgeon.
Distracting things: TV, radio, telephone, playing with my cat.
Benefits: Better grades. Less stress. Feel better about myself.
Goal: To do my homework in my room before I talk on the phone or watch TV.
Time: Weekdays, four to seven P.M. Weekends, Sunday afternoon.
Person: Mom—she knows I want to do better and understands how I feel.

46 *Confidence*

I Know You'll Make the Right Decision

THE SITUATION

You told your parents that you and your girlfriends were going to the movies and coming home right after. Your friends didn't tell you that they were planning on stopping by the party at Alex's on the way home. This was the big rager everyone had been waiting for.

All week long, exclusive invitations were passed around school for Alex Jacobs's seventeenth birthday party. Everyone knew that Alex's parents were the cool type who let him do whatever he wanted. And they were rich too. As long as things didn't get out of hand, his parents let Alex and his friends party at his own home. Tonight was his birthday, and his dad bought him a couple kegs of beer. "Just don't let things get out of hand," his dad told him before going out for the evening.

You really didn't want to go, but what are you supposed to say when you're sitting in the backseat, your house is in the opposite direction, and your friend Nancy, who just also happens to be driving, has a huge crush on Alex? The four of you pull up in front of Alex's house. Thirty to forty kids are hanging outside lacking the necessary credentials to enter, the beating music is pounding from the backyard, and cars are pulling up every few seconds like at a movie premiere. "Come on, let's go," shouts Nancy as she double parks. The four of you hop out of the car and head up the brick walk.

Inside, the beer is flowing, bodies are gyrating next to the pool, and various couples are making out in semi-secluded spots. This is not the place you want to be. This is the scene that has messed up more than a few of your friends, and you know enough to realize this is not what you want in life.

You nervously follow your friends through the living room, saying hi to a couple people along the way, when all of a sudden you spy a portable telephone in the kitchen. Your friends go left toward the keg, and you head right to the phone in the kitchen. About ten people are in the kitchen, so it's too loud to talk. You pick up the receiver, step into the laundry room next to the kitchen, and dial home. "Hello," answers your mom. What do you say?

THE SCRIPTURE

For we do not have a high priest who is unable to sympathize with our weaknesses, but we have one who has been tempted in every way, just as we are—yet was without sin. Let us then approach the throne of grace with confidence, so that we may receive mercy and find grace to help us in our time of need.
Hebrews 4:15–16

The right decision isn't always the most desirable decision to make. Making right decisions means having to stand up to your friends sometimes. Making right decisions means having to explain why you're leaving a party when there are so many cute guys around. Making a right decision may mean not pulling up to the beautiful lookout spot over the moonlit water with your girlfriend.

Good parents are the ones who coach you how to make right decisions. The situations you encounter may not always seem to have a black and white, right or wrong decision attached to them. Like parties: Do you stay to try to convince your friends not to drink, or do you call your folks to pick you up before the cops get there and you really get busted? Sometimes there are a lot of right things to do, and other times your choices are limited so you make the best one possible and hope it'll make sense when you explain it to your parents.

As a teenager, there are a zillion choices that you and you alone can make. Your parents can help you to know how to make good choices, but what you do is ultimately up to you. It takes confidence to make good, hard decisions. That's why it's encouraging to know that even though Jesus was tempted in every way, he still had what it took to make good decisions. He understands when you're faced with a lot of temptations. He knows what it's like to be pulled in the wrong direction. When you're faced with difficult choices, God's grace will be just what you need to make the right decision.

THE STRATEGY

What difficult decisions are you facing this week? Which friendships are pulling you in the wrong direction? What temptations seem to be getting the upper hand in your heart? Read the story of the temptation of Jesus in Matthew 4 and see how Jesus handled the temptations Satan threw at him. Know that Jesus can handle any temptation that's too big for you. Finish your time alone with God by reading 1 Corinthians 10:13, and know that God will provide a way out for you so you can keep walking with him.

47 Prayer

I'm Praying for You

THE SITUATION

Whenever my sisters, brother, or I had an important athletic event, test, school performance, trip, or other upcoming challenge, my mom would always let us know she was praying for us. As she hugged and kissed us, sending us on our way, she'd say, "I'll say a prayer for you." If we were stressed about an upcoming exam or being in the finals of a competition, she always reminded us, "Don't forget to say a prayer."

My dad headed out early a few mornings every week to go to morning Mass at St. Edward's. In the afternoon on game days, he'd take off work early to make it to our matches. Standing on the sidelines, he and my mom would always be there to support us. Whether we won or lost didn't really matter because Mom and Dad were always there regardless of the final score. We didn't need a band, drill team, or cheerleaders: We had Mom and Dad.

Whether holding a volleyball getting ready to serve, running with hands outstretched to receive a throw, singing in a play, playing quarterback in the powder puff football game, or heading to the finish line in track, we knew our folks were always praying for us. My mom always let us know that she was praying for us. My dad wasn't as vocal, but we knew he had said his prayers for us earlier that day at church. What their prayers didn't get us in the way of points sure did inspire us in a way of life. Every time Mom and Dad prayed for us, it made a difference. How much of a difference? I don't exactly know. But hearing over and over that someone was praying for me was enough to change my life.

THE SCRIPTURE

> Pray continually.
> 1 Thessalonians 5:17

My parents never stopped praying for our family. Mom and Dad prayed continually. They never ceased to pray, because they knew that prayer changes people.

When your parents tell you that they're praying for you, that means you are receiving major air support from the power of God. Over and over, the Bible commands Christians to pray. To never stop praying. To pray in the morning. To pray at night. To pray for loved ones. To pray for enemies. To pray for rulers, kings, queens, and government officials. To pray for the poor and oppressed. To pray for widows and orphans. To pray for people who don't know Jesus Christ. To pray during good times. To pray during bad times. The Bible tells us to pray, pray, pray.

Shadowlands is a movie about the life of the famous Christian writer, C. S. Lewis. In the movie, Lewis's wife is dying of cancer, but after a period of treatment she begins to recover. When C. S. Lewis's friends hear of the cancer's remission, one of them says, "Well, it appears that God seems to be hearing your prayers." C. S. Lewis eagerly replies, "I don't pray in order for God to answer my prayers. I don't pray to change God or change his mind. *I pray because prayer changes me!"* (Emphasis added.)

Praying for another person is a privilege, and if your folks are praying for you, it's likely that they're drawing closer to God in the process. As your parents and others pray for you, what's important is not how many touchdowns are scored or how many notes are hit on key. What is most important is that you draw closer to God. That will change your life.

THE STRATEGY

Some of you may be wondering, *This is great, but my parents don't pray for me. My parents don't even know God. What am I supposed to do?* Pray. You can be a very positive influence in your parents' lives by praying for them on a regular basis. I've known many parents who have come to faith in Christ because their teenage son or daughter was praying for them. Whether your parents are praying for you or not, study these verses to discover what God says about the life-changing importance of prayer.

> I pray that you may be active in sharing your faith, so that you will have a full understanding of every good thing we have in Christ.
>
> Philemon 6

> Therefore let everyone who is godly pray to you
>   while you may be found;
> surely when the mighty waters rise,
>   they will not reach him.
>
> Psalm 32:6

> But I pray to you, O LORD,
>   in the time of your favor;

in your great love, O God,
    answer me with your sure salvation.
                                    Psalm 69:13

Then you will call upon me and come and pray to me, and
I will listen to you.
                                    Jeremiah 29:12

This, then, is how you should pray:

"Our Father in heaven,
hallowed be your name,
your kingdom come,
your will be done
    on earth as it is in heaven.
Give us today our daily bread.
Forgive us our debts,
    as we also have forgiven our debtors.
And lead us not into temptation,
but deliver us from the evil one."
                                    Matthew 6:9–13

In all my prayers for all of you, I always pray with joy. . . .
                                    Philippians 1:4

One of those days Jesus went out to a mountainside to pray,
and spent the night praying to God.
                                    Luke 6:12

. . . bless those who curse you, pray for those who mistreat
you.
                                    Luke 6:28

Blessing

God Bless You

THE SITUATION

There's a little four-year-old girl in my life that I'm very fond of. Her name's Janae and she's my daughter. As you well know by now, I have all sorts of wild and crazy memories about growing up in a large family, but the fun hasn't stopped there. Janae and I do all sorts of wild and crazy things together.

For instance, right now the big rage with kids is the Disney movie *Aladdin*. In our home, located in the ancient city of Agraba, I have multiple personalities: I'm the Daddy of the Lamp, Prince Ali, Abu the monkey, Raja the tiger, Iago the parrot, and Jafar, the evil court "vestir." Janae only wants to play one character: She's Princess Jasmine.

Besides playing Aladdin, Janae likes to play flashlight hide-n-seek, read book after book, listen to her music tapes, cre ate forts with sheets, pillows, and blankets, wrestle with me (she has a mean WWF kneedrop to the chest), and do gymnastics on our king-size bed. Janae is never lacking in energy or creativity. She's also a budding theologian. Recently we were talking about her love of waffles. I gave her a typical parental comment saying, "Janae, if you eat one more waffle, you're going to turn into a waffle." Janae shot back, "Daddy, people can't turn into waffles." She stopped for a moment and then said, "But if Jesus wants to, he can turn into a waffle." Can Jesus turn into a waffle? If God could become flesh, I guess he could also become Bisquick batter.

One of the favorite parts of my day is sneaking into Janae's room after she has gone to sleep. Kneeling beside her bed and covering her with the covers she always uncovers herself with, I put my hand on her head and pray for God's blessing on her life. I thank God for the happiness he has blessed me with in such a fun and loving daughter. I pray that Janae will always know and experience God's love deeply. I pray for God to protect, guide, and direct every step of her next day. I also pray for the strength to be a loving and humble daddy. And I ask God to give me his love so I can be a consistently caring and sensitive father who loves Janae at all times, at all cost, and in all ways. That's a tall order, but that's the blessing I pray Janae will know every day of her life. No blessing is too big for God.

THE SCRIPTURE

> The LORD bless you
> and keep you;
> the LORD make his face shine upon you
> and be gracious to you;
> the LORD turn his face toward you
> and give you peace.
> Numbers 6:24–26

Receiving a blessing from your parents is probably the most important gift you could ever receive. The words "God bless you" are far more than a trite phrase, an American political saying, or a protection against your heart stopping after you sneeze. "God bless you" is an outpouring of all the goodness of God into your life. It is a blessing you can never get enough of.

In the old days, receiving a blessing from one's parents was extremely important. A blessing signified a father's love and affirmation toward his children. A blessing ensured that the children received the father's inheritance after he was dead and gone. A blessing was a sign of favor, a demonstration of love. The opposite of a blessing was a curse, and that was something you definitely wanted to avoid. A curse meant you were cut off from the family, never to receive any of the benefits or privileges of being a family member. Receiving a blessing was so important that brothers actually fought over receiving blessings from their father (see Gen. 27).

A blessing is your parents' unconditional love for, acceptance of, and belief in you. You may still get in arguments and fights with your folks, but that doesn't mean you can't receive or haven't received their blessing yet. Whatever you go after in life, be sure to go after your parents' blessing. A blessing can change your life.

THE STRATEGY

You may not be sure if you've received a blessing from your folks or not. Sometimes they're cool to you; other times they're not, so how can you be sure? Here's a risky but worthwhile thing to do: Ask your mom and dad to read this chapter and discuss it with you. It may help them realize just how important their role in your life is. Ask your folks to give you their blessing by praying for you and telling you of their unconditional love for you. I realize this sounds really heavy, but receiving your parents' blessing may be the very thing that helps improve your relationship with them.

For People Who Know They Don't Have Their Parents' Blessing

Some parents are screwed up. If that's your parents, then you and I know that the chance of receiving anything from them is zero. My prayer for you is that you have an older person in your life, besides a girlfriend or boyfriend, who deeply loves and cares for you. A grandparent, uncle, youth pastor, coach, or aunt is a person who can be a significant role model for you. If you're not sure of one, know that God loves you more than you could ever imagine; but I also hope that there's someone in your life who's a close second to him. Sit down with that person and talk about this whole idea of receiving a blessing. If nobody comes to mind, then you can call me and I'll talk with you, pray with you, and give you my blessing. Call me at (714) 581-6681. I'd love to encourage you and see God accomplish his great plan for your life.

49 Affirmation

I Believe in You

THE SITUATION

"What's going on here?" my dad asked as he walked down the driveway.

"He says I stole his seventy-five dollars . . . I didn't steal anything," I cried.

"That boy had better return every penny he stole from me. He's not allowed back into this house until he does," the old man shouted at my dad.

"Pipe down! He didn't steal any of your money. He says he didn't and I believe him," my dad yelled back at the old man.

I was in seventh grade. I had been playing at a friend's house across the street just like I had every day for years. His parents were gone, and the grandparents were left in charge to baby-sit. All day long kids had been running in and out of the house. We were all in the kitchen when Bill's grandpa walked in and lifted his bony finger at me, saying, "Where's the seventy-five dollars I had sitting on this counter?"

Is he talking to me? I wondered.

The old man looked right at me and asked the same question again, only this time a little bit louder, with anger coming through loud and clear.

"Seventy-five dollars? I didn't take any money . . . I don't know what you're talking about," I stammered, embarrassed and wondering why I was singled out as a thief.

He started moving closer to me. The other guys backed away.

"Listen to me, young man! I left seventy-five dollars on this counter and you're the only one in the kitchen who saw it here. Now give me back my money!"

Has this guy been smoking denture toothpaste, or what? I didn't know what in the world he was talking about. I hadn't seen any money anywhere, and I had been with the guys all afternoon. Intimidated and scared, I slowly backed away, heading for the door as he began to chase me down. A pursuit ensued.

He ran after me screaming, "You're not allowed back into this house until you give back every dollar you stole!" Just then my dad pulled into our driveway.

I ran up to my dad screaming and crying about the old man's accusations. That's when Dad stepped in and silenced the old man. My dad, the hero.

THE SCRIPTURE

What, then, shall we say in response to this? If God is for us, who can be against us?

Romans 8:31

Being accused of something you didn't do gives you the worst feeling in the world. It gives you this deep, raw, stomach-churning, bile-producing feeling like you're going to throw up. If you try to deny stealing seventy-five dollars, then you look guilty. If you say nothing, then you look guilty. Since you're the one being accused, your testimony doesn't count for much. That's why you need either witnesses, which I didn't have, or someone to testify on your behalf, which I did have.

When my dad stood up to that old man for me that day in the middle of the street, he gave me the greatest affirmation I could ever receive. I needed someone to believe in me when no one else did. My friends had left me. No one stood up for me but my dad.

When my dad said he believed me and not the old man, he wasn't only saying that he didn't think I took the money, but more importantly, he was saying that *he believed in me.* Believing in someone is one of the most powerful ways to show that you love them. My dad demonstrated his love for me by believing in me. He stood by me to face the false accusations I couldn't face on my own.

When your mom or dad says, "I believe in you," you are receiving a wonderful gift that will last you all the days of your life. Knowing that someone believes in you and stands up for you when no one else does will create the confidence and courage to handle any hardship or problem that comes your way.

Maybe no one has ever said that they believe in you. Maybe your mom or dad have said a lot of hurtful, negative words to you instead of encouraging, positive words. If that's the position you're in, then I've got good news for you: God is saying to you today, "I believe in you." You see, God believes in you when no one else does, including yourself. He is the one who will stand up for you every single minute of the day. Knowing that God believes in you, you can receive confidence and courage even when facing fears and doubts. If God is for you, who can possibly be against you?

THE STRATEGY

Are you feeling defeated? Do you feel like a loser or a discouraged and hopeless louse? Everyone has days when nothing seems to go right and no one understands what you're going through. The person who believes in you is right by your side, and that person is God. He believes in you regardless of what you've done or what others have done to you. Spend some time alone with God thinking about these verses. Thank God for the encouragement he gives you through his Word. Commit your life and problems to him today, knowing that he promises never to leave you or forsake you.

> Be strong and courageous. Do not be afraid or terrified because of them, for the LORD your God goes with you; he will never leave you nor forsake you.
>
> Deuteronomy 31:6

> And we know that in all things God works for the good of those who love him, who have been called according to his purpose.
>
> Romans 8:28

> The LORD is my rock, my fortress and my deliverer;
> my God is my rock, in whom I take refuge.
> He is my shield and the horn of my salvation, my stronghold.
>
> Psalm 18:2

> But you, O Lord, are a compassionate and gracious God,
> slow to anger, abounding in love and faithfulness.
>
> Psalm 86:15

> But God demonstrates his own love for us in this: While we were still sinners, Christ died for us.
>
> Romans 5:8

50   Love

I Love You

THE SITUATION

One Guy Didn't

Three guys were tried for crimes against humanity.
Two guys committed crimes.
One guy didn't.

Three guys were given government trials.
Two guys had fair trials.
One guy didn't.

Three guys were whipped and beaten.
Two guys had it coming.
One guy didn't.

Three guys were given crosses to carry.
Two guys earned their crosses.
One guy didn't.

Three guys were mocked and spit at along the way.
Two guys cursed and spit back.
One guy didn't.

Three guys were nailed to crosses.
Two guys deserved it.
One guy didn't.

Three guys agonized over their abandonment.
Two guys had reason to be abandoned.
One guy didn't.

Three guys talked while hanging on their crosses.
Two guys argued.
One guy didn't.

Three guys knew death was coming.
Two guys resisted.
One guy didn't.

One.
Two.
Three guys died on three crosses.

Three days later.
Two guys remained in their graves.
One guy didn't.

THE SCRIPTURE

But God demonstrates his own love for us in this: While we
were still sinners, Christ died for us.

Romans 5:8

Parents say crazy things because they love you. I know it's
a crazy way to show that they love you, but they're the only
parents you have. If your parents love you in such crazy ways,
then what about God? Is God crazy about you too? Why
would God want to love you and me? Why would God love
us when our lives are filled with mistakes, broken promises,
poor decisions, and selfish sins? Why would God choose to
love a planet filled with people who run from him?

That's an almost impossible question to answer, so the
only one to answer it is God himself. He says that while we
were still sinners, his one and only Son, Jesus, died for us.
Why? Love. Even though you and I willfully said "Hasta
luego" to God, he still chose to love us. Is God crazy or what?

God has an adventurous, dangerous love for you. Over and
over again he says, "I love you." Even when he gets hurt, he
still loves you. He doesn't ignore the truth about your sin, but
because he loves you, he sent Jesus so you could know the truth
and the truth could set you free. You see, God can't stop thinking about you. You are on his mind day and night. God's love
for you is not temporary like that of an infatuated friend. His
love is not conditional like that of a friend who sticks around
depending on what you do for him. His love is not selfish like
that of a friend who looks out for her interests only. His love is

faithful, unconditional, and eternal. He has always loved you and always will. There is nothing you can do to earn his love and acceptance because he accepts you the way you are. I know it sounds crazy (because it is), but God loves you. He created you so you can have a life-changing relationship with him.

When Jesus died on a cross for your sins, he was looking in two directions, heaven and hell. He could have called the whole thing off, but he was looking both ways for you. He finally yelled to his Father, who watched from heaven, "It is finished," and took his last breath. Jesus died on a lonely cross and rose from the dead three days later because of his great love for you. When you wake up every morning and think about your day, consider Jesus, who looked both ways. It's not as crazy as it sounds: *Look both ways.*

THE STRATEGY

God's love for you can change your life if you allow his Spirit to work in it. Take a sheet of paper and draw a line down the center. At the top of the left half, write "My Way." At the top of the right half, write "God's Way." List the different problems you face and feelings you have about what's happening in your life. In the "My Way" column, write down how you usually handle things in your own power. In the "God's Way" column, write down what the Bible says is God's way to handle conflicts. How can you make your way God's way? How can you look both ways in every situation so you can be the person God wants you to be? Who can help you with these areas of struggle in your life? Close your time in prayer asking God to help you look both ways in every thought and decision you make. Not only will he help you to look both ways, he'll give you the power and strength to choose his way over your way.

> Humble yourselves, therefore, under God's mighty hand, that he may lift you up in due time. Cast all your anxiety on him because he cares for you.
>
> 1 Peter 5:6–7